DARLENE LUNSFORD

MOON OVER PENDER HARBOR

by Darlene Lunsford

I am so grateful:

To God, Who makes all things possible!

To my friends and family for reading my first book;

To Cynthia Hickey and Winged Publications for believing in me;

And to my Luns, for your love, your support, your encouragement, and your ideas for future books!

"My heart overfloweth with a goodly matter; I speak the things which I have made touching the king: My tongue is the pen of a ready writer."

Psalm 45:1, American Standard Version

ALL PROCEEDS FROM MY BOOK SALES WILL GO TO Togo Literature, the literature center in Togo (West Africa). This ministry exists to strengthen the church in Togo by providing literature in French and local languages at affordable prices to Togolese, other West Africans, and missionaries who work with nationals.

i

Chapter One

A sliver of light from a full moon beamed through the bedroom window of the little cabin. Alexis rolled out of bed as quietly as possible so not to wake Cliff, her husband of two years. Stepping into the pink fuzzy slippers he had given her last Christmas, she groped along the dark hallway to the bathroom and switched on the light. She glanced in the mirror at her unsmiling reflection, chin-length blonde hair uncombed and wide-set blue eyes looking very weary, not so much from the early hour as from life's stresses. At 22, she had a youthful figure from healthy living and daily activities at the harbor, her home since she was a child. But the ever-present happy gleam in her eyes had disappeared over the last couple of months.

Alexis shivered, already missing the warmth of the down comforter on the double bed. This was proving to be more difficult than she had thought. Quickly she brushed her teeth and applied light makeup. After running a brush through her hair, she walked back into the bedroom and glanced over at Cliff, deep asleep. Dark, unruly chestnut-brown hair matted the pillow. The bedcovers had fallen from his shoulders, leaving his broad back exposed. Alexis quickly turned away, pushing aside a strong urge to kiss him goodbye. Her instincts told her that to hesitate would mean the demise of her well-planned arrangements. If Cliff knew what she was about to do, he would use his best efforts to keep her from leaving.

Resigned to the task at hand, Alexis noiselessly pulled on her jeans, then sweatshirt and tennis shoes. Opening the closet door, she pulled out the little green suitcase, already packed with the few necessities a two-week stay would require. She grabbed her shoulder bag from the chair and slowly withdrew the envelope containing a carefully drafted letter. With a heavy sigh, she walked out to the kitchen and placed the envelope in a conspicuous place on the table.

Her moment had arrived. Without looking back, Alexis opened the front door and walked into the moonlight.

The sea-blue 17-foot Seaswirl gently sloshed back and forth in the dark water of Pender Harbor, which looked much more ominous at five-thirty in the morning than Alexis had ever seen it. She had been out this early before, heading for her favorite fishing spot-- but never alone, and never without someone aware of her whereabouts. This particular morning no one knew, and no one *would* know, if she were careful. Alexis hesitated a second, reconsidering, then remembered the last big argument with Cliff that had led to her departure. In an hour he would awaken. She must go, NOW, before she lost her nerve. She had to get away, at least for a while. From Pender Harbor. From the resort she and Cliff ran along with her parents. From her mom and dad. From Cliff.

Life at the Canadian fishing resort her parents ran was the only life Alexis had known for most of her life. As a five-year-old her dad patiently taught her to fish, and she was baiting her own hooks at six. She learned how to maneuver a boat in and out of the harbor before taking her driver's test. Days were busy with fishing and crabbing, evenings filled with salmon bakes and fish frys with the guests.

That life had been fine for a while. *When did it all change?* Alexis mused. *Why couldn't I have been happy with the way things were?*

As she had done so many times before, Alexis untied the rope from the cleat, then jumped on board the boat she had grown to love. She pushed away from the dock with one oar, then gradually eased into the current, starting the motor only after the boat was around the bend. As the motor began its familiar sputter and the Seaswirl skimmed easily over the dark water, Alexis smiled, remembering the first and only other time she had left in a boat without saying goodbye.

* * *

Chapter Two

Alexis first met Cliff when she was twelve. At fifteen, he was a skinny kid, his bare chest white as a fish belly from lack of exposure, his arms thin and gangly. Her first sight of Cliff was him standing on the dock with a fishing pole in both hands, trying to untangle the line from a mass of seaweed. He flicked stringy brown hair out of his eyes as, annoyed, he jerked his pole back and forth.

Alexis sat in her father Charlie's boat, a 17-foot sea-blue Seaswirl which was the envy of many of her father's friends. The boat was tied loosely to the dock, with Alexis's fishing line dangling over the edge into the water. Her soft, honey-blonde curls were tucked up inside a red fishing cap to hide any tell-tale hint of femininity. The bright yellow T-shirt she wore was filthy from cleaning fish, one of her favorite pastimes. From her position, Alexis watched him for a while, amused, until he looked over and caught her eye. Apparently, the boy, whom she had never seen before, did not like being stared at, for he suddenly yelled, "Hey, kid! What are you doing in Charlie's boat?"

Startled, and annoyed at his rudeness, Alexis pulled on the throttle and started the engine. She tugged on the rope until it came loose from the cleat and drove away from the dock with an exultant glance in the boy's direction. He stood glaring after her, and she watched him drop the pole on the dock and sprint up the hill, presumably to tell her father. When Alexis arrived home later that day, she was grounded for two weeks for taking the boat without her father's consent.

Having no brothers, Alexis did not know how to treat boys. At first, she ignored the newcomer, whom she soon learned was Cliff Hunter, visiting with his aunt and uncle from Alaska. But when he started taking her place as dock hand, she became furious. The afternoon Alexis caught him selling live bait to the guests she stormed up to her father, ignoring the fact that he was in mid-conversation with one of the male guests.

"Dad," she sputtered, "why are you letting that boy sell herring to the fishermen? That's supposed to be *my* job!"

"Excuse me, Mr. Hunter," Charlie said to the man, clearly irritated with his only child. "Yes, Alexis, what *is* it?" His dark eyebrows furrowed, but the visitor appeared slightly amused.

Hands on hips, Alexis explained the situation. "That kid is taking over all my jobs! I caught him at the gas pumps earlier today and now he's selling bait! He--"

She would have continued had her father not raised a hand to stop her. "You had better get used to 'that kid', Alexis, because I was just talking to his uncle here about offering him a job." He crossed his arms against his broad chest and frowned at her. "Besides, it will give you more time to help your mother. As for now, I don't really care WHO does the work around here, AS LONG AS IT GETS DONE!" He glared at her as Cliff's uncle held a hand against his mouth to hide a smile.

"And Alexis," her father called as she turned to leave, "GO CHANGE THAT DIRTY SHIRT!"

Furious, Alexis stomped up to the house. Pumping gas, catching herring to be used as live bait by the fishermen, tying up the boats, and cleaning fish for the customers--those had all been her jobs! *Especially* cleaning the fish. Working on the docks was certainly more fun than helping her mother with household drudgery.

Slamming the door behind her, Alexis stormed into the house, heading for her room and a clean shirt.

"Alexis, honey, is that you?" her mother called, entering the living room with a basket of fresh laundry in her arms. "Fold these towels and put them away, will you?"

Huffing, Alexis took the basket and disappeared into the bathroom. Kate smiled and shook her head, brushing an ash-blonde hair from her brow. Something had obviously gone wrong in her young daughter's life for her to suddenly appear at the house in the middle of a hot summer afternoon. Later Kate would find out exactly what. Right now, she needed to get back to the resort's office, as she could see a car pulling up outside.

Running the fishing resort kept the entire family busy. During fall and winter months when business was slow, Charlie tended the registration desk. Kate changed beds, washed sheets and towels, and cleaned rooms, as well as doing all of the cooking, cleaning and laundry for her own family. When Alexis was old enough, Kate started training her to assist, but to Alexis the work was a tedious chore. She preferred the smelly life of the docks to the calmer domestic duties. The issue was a continual source of discord between her and her mother. About the only part of maid service Alexis liked was the tips the guests left behind which her parents allowed her to keep to save for a new fishing pole.

In the spring and summer months the family hired temporary help to keep up the 16 units, which included four motel rooms, eight cabins, two single-wide mobile homes and two small cottages. Kate worked in the office while Charlie maintained the units and the grounds, assisting the fishermen with whatever they needed. Alexis usually disappeared in the morning and did not reappear until suppertime.

That particular summer was no exception. Alexis pretended not to mind that Cliff took over her jobs, as well as, apparently, her father's good graces. She spent many carefree hours lazing about on the dock in her swimsuit, and even more hour's fishing. When Cliff decided to stop ignoring her and challenged her to who could catch the bigger fish, she triumphantly reeled in a 14-inch Rock Cod to his 12-inch. The minor victory seemed to win Cliff's respect, and fishing together became an everyday event.

By the end of that first summer, Cliff was tanned and muscular, a natural result of hours in the sun pulling boats out of the water and chopping firewood for the guests. He had earned the attention and respect of her father, who, true to his word, offered Cliff a job if he returned the next year. When it came time for Cliff and his uncle and aunt to head home to Alaska, Alexis even felt a little sorry to see him go. He wasn't bad, she told herself--for a boy.

Cliff worked the following summer, and the one after that. As the months and years progressed, he and Alexis became close friends without realizing what was happening. After arguments with her parents, Alexis would confide in Cliff. When neither of them had responsibilities, they borrowed her father's Seaswirl and went fishing or for a boat ride down the inlet. Her parents trusted Cliff implicitly--with their boat or with their daughter.

He teased her constantly, dubbing her "little Alex" and ruffling her hair until she became annoyed. But he seemed different than other boys. His competitiveness attracted her; rather than treating her like a helpless female, he continually challenged her to do better. With his dry sense of humor, he kept them both laughing until their sides hurt.

Cliff left for college when he was eighteen. As Alexis watched him drive away, the realization dawned on her that she was in love with him. Yes, he had won her heart. And he didn't even know it. At fifteen, Alexis was still considered just a kid by the soon-to-be collegiate. She sighed. Her father had reminded Cliff that the job was his as long as he wanted it. Cliff said he would let Charlie know as soon as he could give him a definite answer but had no idea what the future would hold.

Alexis kept her fingers crossed. She knew he would be back. He just *had* to be.

* * *

Chapter Three

After that first year of college Cliff did come back to the harbor, pleasantly surprised at the changes in Alexis. Her blonde hair was no longer tucked up inside a cap but loosely brushed her shoulders. A few freckles sprinkled across her nose, and her blue eyes sparkled with good health, giving her the fresh look of someone who spent a lot of time outdoors. Curves appeared in all the right places, and instead of a skinny kid, she was fast becoming a young woman.

"Where's little Alex?" Cliff asked in a husky voice, ruffling her hair as he had always done. He had retrieved his overnight bag from the Blazer and stood looking down at her.

A tingle went through her body. The familiar gesture would in time past have irritated her, but now she melted at his touch. His shoulders were broader than she remembered, his eyes just as dark and brooding, his hair needing a hand to gently brush it out of his face. Just being near him took her breath away, but as he spoke, she tried to hide her excitement at his return.

Suddenly shy, she offered him a slow smile. "Little Alex is here, but she's not so little anymore." Then, wanting to break the silence, she asked, "How was college?"

He shrugged. "It's a whole different life than the harbor, that's for sure. Sometimes my brain felt like it would burst if it held any more information! I'm looking forward to working with my hands for a while, not my mind." His eyes challenged her. "You ready to give up all your smelly jobs?"

Alexis grinned. "Don't worry, I won't fight you for them. Mom has me tending the office these days. It's still better than maid service--except for the tips!" A compromise had been reached when Alexis decided she enjoyed greeting the customers, assigning them rooms, and collecting the money. Now that she was older and more responsible, she made dependable clerical help. When someone needed a fishing license she could assist them with the registration, and if a customer asked about a good restaurant, Alexis was quick with a recommendation. She and her mother were both happy with the arrangement. Her mother had more time for cooking and bookkeeping, as well as keeping company with the guests, many of whom were now old friends. And Alexis was thrilled to have finally worked herself totally out of maid service.

"Who does all your old jobs when I'm not around?" Cliff teased, turning to walk toward the big house.

Alexis shrugged as she walked slowly along beside him. "Dad, mostly. I still help out with boats since the office is so near the water. On a good day I can even throw a pole over the dock and watch for customers at the same time! And," she added, "I'm the first to see the catch of day and hear the fishermen's yarns."

She gave him an impish smile. What she didn't mention was that tending the office also gave her a chance to read a good romance novel between customers. Or do her nails. Or just sit and daydream, mostly about him.

Alexis turned sixteen a week after Cliff arrived. The day before her birthday, he sauntered into the office and pulled a Coke out of the cooler, which had become his daily practice. Leaning over the counter, he surprised her by saying, "I understand someone's having a birthday tomorrow. What's on your wish list this year, little Alex? A new fishing rod? Or have you been saving your 'maid' money for that?"

She blushed for probably the first time ever and responded tartly, "My wish? No, it's that boys will start treating me like a lady!"

"Ah, well, my princess," Cliff answered, standing up and pretending to be offended. He reached across the counter and gently took her hand in his, lifting it to his lips and kissing her wrist. "A lady, now, eh? And would the lady care to go to dinner with a smelly old fisherman on the eve of her birthday?"

Alexis caught her breath. He was asking her for a date, just like in the books. And since she had never before been asked, she had no idea if her parents would allow it.

"The lady will have to think it over," she replied, attempting a casual attitude but realizing that her hand was shaking. Then, taking in his shirtless appearance, she remarked, "And the gentleman will of course have to be properly dressed."

Cliff threw back his head and laughed. "Is that a 'yes'?"

Alexis hesitated. "Maybe. Can I let you know later today?"

Cliff's eyes twinkled as he released her hand. "Yes, but please don't keep a gentleman waiting too long. Or even a smelly fisherman. There are other fish in the sea, you know."

"There are other fishermen, too," Alexis said haughtily.

Cliff laughed, then turned on his heels and strode through the office door.

Alexis's heart pounded wildly in her chest. Her mind spinning, she left the office unattended for a few moments and bounded toward the house to find her mother.

"Mom!" she yelled as she burst in the front door.

"Alexis, what *is* it?" Kate glanced up from her papers, alarmed at the midday appearance of her daughter. "Is something wrong?"

"Cliff just asked me for a date! Can I go?" Alexis asked, breathless from her sprint up the hill.

"Right now? You mean to go fishing?"

"No, Mom, I mean a *real* date," Alexis explained impatiently, still bewildered at Cliff's invitation. "To dinner--tomorrow night on my birthday!"

Kate frowned thoughtfully. "Hmmm. Well, we had planned a birthday dinner here for you...I could invite him if--"

"Mom, *please*." Alexis's eyes begged. "Could--" She didn't want to hurt her mother's feelings. "Maybe, could the family have a birthday lunch instead?"

Understanding came into her mother's eyes. "I'll talk to your father, dear. Meanwhile, you had better get back to the office."

Back behind the desk, Alexis could think of little else all afternoon. She hoped and prayed her parents would agree to let her go. They had asked her to wait until she was sixteen to date, even though many of the young women in town were double dating at fourteen or even earlier. She knew her mother was protective of her, Alexis being the tomboy she was, and she normally didn't mind. But this was *Cliff*! And it *was* her sixteenth birthday! Besides, her mother had always insisted on her dating only Christian boys--and Cliff had told her once that he had accepted the Lord in vacation Bible school when he was seven. Plus, he attended church with them most Sundays, which pleased her parents. Well, she could only wait for their decision.

To Alexis's delight, her parents agreed. After an early birthday celebration with her family the next evening, Cliff called for her at the front door of the spacious waterfront home. Alexis waited in the living room among her gift wrappings, unaware that most young women would have entered the room after the boy arrived so not to appear overly anxious. She only knew she couldn't wait a minute longer to talk to him, to look across the table into his dark brown eyes, to hear him laugh, to catch up on all the news of the past year. And to have him all to herself for a few hours.

"Evening, Charlie," Cliff nodded in greeting to her father. "Evening, Mrs. Ryan."

"Evening, Cliff," her parents answered in unison.

Glancing at his date, dressed in fresh cotton pants and a shirt that had no stains, Cliff's eyes showed approval. "You ready, Alex?"

She nodded.

"Have fun, Alexis," said her mother. "Be home by ten, we have an early day tomorrow."

"Okay. Bye Mom, Dad," Alexis called over her shoulder as Cliff opened the front door. Just before leaving, she turned around and called, "Thanks for all the birthday presents!"

Outside, Cliff gave her a quick look up and down. "You look almost grown up," he teased. "New outfit?"

"Not new. Just not a good one for fishing." Alexis smiled, but wondered when he would stop joking with her and start really *noticing*. She glanced over at him, taking in his appearance. His dark eyes held just a hint of teasing; his hair seemed for the moment to be staying in place. In his tight black jeans and light yellow open-necked golf shirt, which showed off his tan to the max, Cliff looked like he could conquer the world single-handedly. He had definitely conquered her heart.

Cliff had arranged to borrow her father's boat, having cleaned it up a little after their last fishing excursion. He jumped in first and deftly helped her step down in her slender white sandals, then expertly pulled the boat away from the dock.

Alexis grinned at him, her excitement showing. "This is the first time I've ever been in a boat in a dress!" she confessed.

Cliff let out a deep chuckle, then the two fell silent. His cocky attitude had disappeared for the moment, and he seemed almost nervous. Alexis, having read many a romance novel, pondered how romantic it was to be alone, with a boy, in a boat, on a moonlit evening in Pender Harbor. She sighed. They said nothing else to each other on the short ride across the water, content to simply be in each other's company and take in the beauty around them. Alexis glanced over at him and smiled. He smiled back and lifted his eyebrows, as though he didn't quite know what to expect.

They pulled into the next harbor, which was alive with fishermen just coming in with their catch and skiers calling it a day. As Cliff assisted Alexis out of the boat, he became aware of the curious stares of the locals and the guests. The two made a striking pair and were the only ones wearing anything dressier than blue jeans or shorts.

Being a weekday, the Fishermen's Inn was practically empty, and Cliff led her to a table overlooking the water and the beginning of a beautiful sunset. A single red rose in a crystal vase graced the white linen tablecloth. It took only a minute for Alexis to realize that their table was the only one so adorned. The other tables and booths were covered with bright floral plastic cloths, with no vases or flowers. She felt a tingle go all the way down her spine--how romantic! Before she had a chance to say anything, the waitress, a woman they both recognized, walked over to the table. After a curious glance at them both, she handed them menus, then winked at Alexis before walking away. Alexis wrinkled her nose and giggled.

"What's so funny?" Cliff asked. His dark eyes, amused, studied her carefully. Alexis, her heart beating wildly, resisted the urge to reach out and smooth his now windblown hair back into place.

"We're going to make the Pender Harbor gossip grapevine!" she explained. "I can just see it now--they'll probably have us married with kids before we know it!"

Cliff laughed in response, and the awkward silence was broken. "What would you like to eat?" he asked her, opening his menu.

She scanned the page. "I don't know, everything looks good, doesn't it?"

"Do you like shrimp?"

Her eyes widened. "Oh, yes, but--" She started to protest that it was awfully expensive but kept quiet. She had read once that it was poor manners to mention prices on a date. "Yes, I adore shrimp. Do you?"

His eyes twinkled. "I don't know about *adore*, but it's awfully good. Why don't I order for both of us." It was a statement, not a question, for he then called the waitress over and laid down his menu.

The meal was slow in coming, but neither of them minded. Alexis found Cliff to be a charming dinner date, attentive and interesting. After telling her about a funny incident that day, he asked Alexis about her birthday gifts.

"Well," Alexis slowly began, "my parents usually give me presents together. You know, from *both* of them. But this year, Dad gave me my own set of keys to the car on a pretty gold key chain. *And* my own key to the Seaswirl! And Mom bought me perfume and powder. And they both gave me this watch."

"Perfume and powder? For a fisherman like you?" Cliff teased. Alexis blushed, then extended her wrist for him to sniff the new fragrance.

"Like it?" she asked.

He held her wrist under his nose and sniffed, then, working his way up her arm, he pretended to eat her. "Ah, my da-a-a-rling, you smell good enough to devour!"

Alexis shrieked, pulling back her arm. "Then hopefully they'll bring our dinner soon!" She squealed.

As if on cue, the waitress appeared with their tray. As other patrons came and went, and the moon grew full in the sky, the two were oblivious to their surroundings. They ate shrimp dipped in butter, garlic bread and salad, rice pilaf and chocolate cake. Cliff told of his college classes, the numerous times he stayed up all night studying, and the various professors with their personality quirks. Alexis filled him in on the winner of the harbor's fishing derby, the size of the largest fish caught, and the interesting customers she had met while minding the front desk. When Alexis finally took her last sip of Coke and glanced at her watch, she gasped.

"What's the matter?" Cliff asked.

"It's ten already! I'm late on my very first date!" She jumped up from the table, doubly frustrated after realizing she had let it slip that she'd never dated before. "I've got to call Mom! Can I borrow your cell phone?"

Cliff burst out laughing and walked to the counter to pay the cashier. When he returned, Alexis, very relieved handed back his phone and explained that her parents had extended the curfew half an hour. Her father issued a stern warning to be quiet as they docked the boat, though, so not to wake the guests who chose to go to bed early.

The two walked outside into the beautiful moonlit night. Alexis breathed in the warm summer air, savoring every moment. Cliff took her hand to help her into the boat, and she caught her breath. As soon as they were both seated and Cliff had pulled away from the dock, he produced a brightly wrapped gift from under the seat.

"Oh!" Alexis was taken by surprise. Cliff had never given her a gift before, and she had not expected one this year.

"Well, open it, silly." His voice teased, but his dark eyes were serious.

Tearing away the wrap revealed a bright pink plastic container. Lifting the lid, she pulled up a hinged tray. Upon noticing all the little square compartments, Alexis grinned with pleasure. "A tackle box!" she exclaimed.

Cliff threw back his head and gave forth a deep, hearty laugh. "Actually, it's to keep your makeup in," he explained, then sobered. "Do you even wear makeup?"

"Oh, I see--it's--it's lovely," she replied. "Yes, I do. A little." Then she grinned. "But it would make an even better tackle box! Would you mind?"

Cliff chuckled and shook his head in wonder. "A bright pink tackle box," he murmured. "Ah, my little Alex," he said then, almost to himself, "you haven't changed a bit inside." Then, louder, "You can use it for whatever you want. I thought about it for a tackle box, but when I bought it, I figured you probably didn't even fish anymore."

"I'll say I do," she asserted. "As a matter of fact, do you know who placed second in the fishing derby?" Out of a newly acquired modesty she had withheld that little tidbit during their dinner conversation.

"You *didn't*," Cliff protested.

Alexis smiled smugly. "I did!"

"Bet I can beat you tomorrow!"

"Bet you can't!"

"You're on!"

Wistfully, Alexis realized the short ride was almost over and they were very near the harbor. She placed a warning finger to her lips. Cliff nodded, cut the engine, and drifted up to the pilings. Alexis stepped out and began tying the boat while Cliff docked.

"Thanks, Alex." Cliff gave her an appreciative glance. This time she extended a hand to assist him out of the small craft. He took it and held it tightly as they walked slowly up to the house.

"Do you--want to come in?" she asked softly. "Mom and Dad will probably want a full report."

"'Mom and Dad' will most likely be in bed," Cliff replied, a twinkle in his eyes.

"I had a lovely time," she whispered. "Thank you for dinner. And the tackle box."

"My pleasure." After the slightest hesitation, he leaned down to gently touch her lips with his own.

"Happy sweet sixteen, Alex," he whispered, and turned to walk down the hill to his cabin.

Alexis sighed and leaned back against the door frame. Her very first kiss. And from Cliff. The moon over Pender Harbor shone brighter that night than ever before...or was she seeing life through new eyes?

She opened the front door and floated to her room, grateful both her parents were already in bed. At the moment, she did not wish to share her memories with anyone. Lying in bed alone, her mind recalled and savored every minute of her evening with Cliff.

When her mother woke her the next morning, Alexis, smelling blueberry muffins baking, got out of bed without a second call. The three of them rose at six each day and ate breakfast together before leaving the house. Since it very well might be the only meal eaten as a family, it was the time they discussed everything of importance.

That particular morning, the main topic of importance was Alexis's first date. As Alexis buttered a muffin, her mother quizzed her about the evening. Her father, adding a third teaspoonful of sugar to his coffee, pretended not to be overly interested.

"We went to Fishermen's Inn," Alexis reported, recalling the events of the night before. "And Cliff must have made reservations--can you IMAGINE, reservations, at that little place--because our table was the only one with a real cloth tablecloth and napkins, and a red rose! Plus, Cliff told me all about college, and all his classes, and his funny teachers." She frowned. "Do you know he has to stay up all night sometimes just to keep up?" She shook her head. "Poor Cliff."

Her father winked across the table at her mother. "Kate, dear, maybe we ought not to make the boy work so hard. I didn't realize he was losing sleep during the school year."

Kate only smiled.

"Thanks for letting me stay out later," Alexis said, oblivious to her father's sarcasm. "I wasn't even paying attention to the time. Cliff is so interesting. There I was, right in the middle of a sentence, and all of a sudden I looked at my watch!" Since the watch had been her birthday gift from her parents, she wondered if there had been some forethought in that. Alexis had never been one to watch the clock, since usually the sun or her stomach told her what time of day it was!

"I thought I'd be grounded from dating forever!" she admitted. "And Cliff gave me a new tackle box-- actually it's for makeup, but I'm going to use it for all my fishing stuff. And you know," she said dreamily, "he must have bought it during the school year! Because he said when he bought it he didn't know if I fished anymore!" She sighed. The thought of Cliff *thinking* about her that long before her birthday made her tingle.

Her mother suppressed a smile. "I'm glad you had a good time, dear. Cliff is a very nice boy. When you start dating more, you'll be glad your first was someone as nice as him." A wistful look came into her eye. "A girl always remembers her first date."

"Do you?" Alexis asked. "Remember your first date, I mean?"

"Oh, yes," her mother replied. Her eyes narrowed and she stared off into space. "His name was Albert Vinney, and now he runs a gas station in Vancouver. 'Big Al', everyone used to call him. They probably still do! The bully of the harbor. But he was special to me. To the boys he was a tough guy--to me, he was a friend. I'd had a crush on him since I was five years old. And when I was finally old enough to date, he was the first one to ask."

Charlie cleared his throat, and Kate winked at him.

Alexis was quiet for a minute. "I don't know anyone else I'd want to go out with," she said honestly. "Besides, probably no one would ask me."

But they did. Later that summer, Kevin Trask, a boy she knew from church, invited her to the annual bike hike. Douglas Pender, great-grandson of the original founder of the harbor, wanted to take her to the movies. Somehow Alexis felt disloyal to Cliff, but at her mother's urging she accepted. Both boys had been schoolmates since childhood, she reasoned, so what harm could there be? And besides, it wasn't like Cliff *owned* her or something.

Still, she wrestled with her feelings. The conflict within made for a disturbing summer. Cliff seemed not to mind all the attention she received, and Alexis began to wonder if he even cared at all. Work kept him busy from daylight to dusk, and he hardly took time to fish anymore.

In early August, when Kevin took Alexis fishing, she made a startling discovery. She had been comparing the other boys to Cliff--their looks, their laugh, their sense of humor, even how they cast their line into the water. After that day she begged off dates for the rest of the summer, preferring a boat ride down the inlet or a fish fry with her parents and their friends. She even persuaded Cliff to go fishing a few times.

Alexis watched for opportunities to be with Cliff. She decided to pay more attention to her appearance, replacing even her favorite fishing T-shirts with cotton blouses and her frayed cut-offs with bright-colored shorts. One day her mother told her she made an attractive hostess to the harbor's many guests. Alexis blushed. Did her mom know the real reason for the change?

Cliff seemed to develop a strong thirst after all his hard work, and he often wandered into the office for a cold soda from the cooler. Alexis, knowing he would come, sometimes had cookies or strawberry shortcake waiting as well.

"Hmmmm. You make this?" he asked her one afternoon, savoring a mouthful of strawberries and whipped cream.

"Uh huh."

"I thought you hated being in the kitchen."

Alexis shrugged. "It's not so bad. Besides, it helps Mom out." She was grateful a customer came then, and she turned her attention to the desk. If Cliff only knew. She often rose early or stayed up late to prepare a special snack for him. For now, it was the only way she knew to show him how she felt. What was the old adage about the way to a man's heart?

Alexis could guess what her parents were thinking. That Cliff would go away to college and meet someone, marry, and never come back to the harbor. Alexis wasn't blind. She knew it could happen, but she wasn't going to let it go down easy.

The day Cliff had to leave for his second year of college, the two of them went fishing at six in the morning. She poured him a cup of coffee from the thermos and handed it to him.

He accepted it with a smile, his hand touching hers briefly. "Thanks."

"Are you looking forward to college?" she asked quietly.

His eyes were unreadable. "In some ways."

She blinked back tears at the thought of him leaving. Life would be dull without him, that was certain. And who knew what the future would bring? If only she could hold onto these last few precious hours forever.

Cliff seemed quieter than usual, and she wondered if she was boring him. He would probably meet all kinds of interesting girls at school, she feared, and forget all about her. Only time would tell.

That afternoon, his suitcases loaded in the dark blue Blazer, Cliff stood looking down at her. Her parents had already said their goodbyes in the house, so the two were alone. He looked a little uncertain, and opened his mouth to say something, then gave her a quick hug.

"Take care of yourself, little Alex," he said softly.

"You, too," she told him, and tried to smile, but noticed that he wasn't smiling either. She watched as Cliff solemnly climbed into the Blazer and drove away, just before the tears streamed down her cheeks.

Somehow, she made it through the following school year without him. How, she didn't know. Life at Pender Harbor was lonely without Cliff, but at least school, helping her mother, and an occasional date kept her too busy to be bored. She wrote Cliff a letter now and then, with news of the harbor but nothing too personal. He wrote back only a few times, explaining what a heavy class load he had and that he could barely keep up. Alexis kept his letters, placing them carefully in her dresser drawer for safekeeping.

The next summer Cliff arrived as usual, but he seemed distant, their easy comradery gone. Alexis's hopes plummeted. She had so looked forward to his return, and now this. Was he angry at her? The two of them fished together only four or five times, and he hardly ever stopped in the office for drinks. The few desserts she prepared for him went uneaten, so she soon ceased her efforts. Alexis later learned from her father that Cliff had a girlfriend at college. She sadly wondered if things between them would ever be the same.

That fall when he left for college, Alexis doubted he would be back. Finding a job would not be difficult for someone with the computer knowledge and skills he had acquired. He seemed to be outgrowing the harbor as quickly as he was outgrowing her. Alexis did not even get the chance to say goodbye. Not realizing he was leaving so soon, she had offered to do the grocery shopping in town for her mother. When she returned, he was gone.

During her senior year Alexis began to seriously consider her own life's vocation. The decision was not a difficult one -- she had wanted to be a nurse since she was a little girl. While other children squeamishly avoided the dock where men were slicing open their day's catch, Alexis watched the activities with keen interest. She remembered standing nearby and pelleting her father with questions about the inside of a fish belly.

"Daddy, what's that?" she continually asked, and he would patiently explain. When he did not know the answer, he would respond, "I'm not sure--why don't we look it up in a book?" To Alexis's delight, they were always able to find just the right book in the local library, which carefully detailed the inside structure of a fish. As she grew older, her dad taught her how to navigate the internet and search for the answers. Ever since then, Alexis had an eager curiosity about animals, and people, and just what made each intricate system work.

With that in mind, Alexis wrote to the few schools nearby offering a nursing program. By the time high school graduation neared, she had decided on and been accepted at the University of British Columbia for their four-year nursing program.

As life would have it, the same day Alexis's acceptance letter from college arrived in the mail came a letter from Cliff to her parents. He would not be returning to the harbor that year; he hoped they wouldn't have a hard time finding a replacement for him; he wished them the best.

"Replacement," Alexis thought ruefully. As though anyone could ever replace Cliff. She cried for three days, her mom checking on her often. Then, recovering, she threw herself into her studies, took over the laundry duties for her mother, and filled her weekends with activities.

Fortunately, Alexis had become quite active in the church youth group that year, having been voted in as secretary and social planner. Doug Pender was president, and the two spent hours at the home of one or the other brainstorming. The time together resulted in many well-organized activities as well as a mutual attraction. Thanksgiving banquet that fall was the best one they'd ever had, and the bake sale to earn money for painting their meeting room brought in enough to also buy wallpaper. Since they both enjoyed decorating, they were always among the handful of teenagers painting or wallpapering. Alexis even learned how to stencil and stenciled an artistic border all the way around the room.

Douglas Pender shared many of her interests, including fishing, and her parents liked him. So, what was wrong with her? she wondered. Why couldn't she be interested in someone like him? But though he was handsome and fun, as well as a good friend, Alexis's heart was still empty. Tearfully, she broke off their relationship just before leaving for her first year at college.

He just didn't compare to Cliff. Maybe no one ever would.

* * *

Chapter Four

On a glorious autumn day in early September, Alexis's parents drove her to Langdale to catch the ferry. A part of her jumped at the chance to get away, to see life on the other side of the world--or at least, Vancouver. But a week at summer camp several years ago had been the only time away for even a few days, and tears stung her eyes at the thought of leaving. Just before boarding, she gave both of her parents a hug. Her father's craggy face showed weariness, and her mother's eyes were red from crying.

"We love you, honey," Kate told her. "Call if you need anything."

"Make sure the specimens are dead before dissecting them," her father said gruffly in what Alexis knew to be a poor attempt to mask his true feelings. He held Alexis tightly for a few moments before releasing her.

As the ferry pulled away, loud horns blaring, Alexis stood on the deck waving, tears running down her face. This was goodbye to her childhood--she was now taking the first step to her future. In four years, she would be a nurse, a profession that could take her anywhere in the world.

With or without Cliff Hunter.

When the ferry arrived at Horseshoe Bay, Alexis looked for a cab and found several waiting. Since her parents only owned one car, cabs and buses would have to suffice for transportation for the year. She hoped to catch occasional rides to town with friends at school.

"Where to?" the driver asked.

"University of British Columbia," she responded, then sat back in her seat to enjoy the sights. She was wearing one of the new outfits she had purchased for school, olive-green pants with a matching V-neck jacket with tortoise-look buttons. Considering Alexis hardly ever left the harbor, she felt quite stylish and grown up. For the present she tried to forget about leaving home and concentrate only on the adventures that lie ahead.

The driver kept up a running conversation with her as they drove past Stanley Park and over the Lions Gate Bridge, then through the busy city of Vancouver. Alexis had been to Vancouver only a few times and was awed at the tall bank buildings and many shopping centers. People of all shapes and sizes and nationalities waited on street corners for the light to change or walked brusquely down the busy street.

"Say, do you happen to have a bus schedule?" Alexis asked the cabby, reminded by the sight of the many bus stops.

"I sure do, ma'am," he responded, obviously priding himself on the fact that he was ready for every occasion. Keeping his eyes carefully on the road, he flipped down the sun visor on the passenger's side and pulled out a brightly colored brochure. Handing it back to her, he asked, "Going to be using the buses a lot?"

"At least a couple times a month, most likely," she told him. "I'm sure I'll be too busy to come to the city very often, though, and there is a small supply store on campus."

They soon left the city behind and headed through quieter residential areas. The driver said no more to her until pulling up outside the solemn gray building which bore the words "Administration Building."

"We're here, miss," he told her. After turning off the motor, the cabby got out and unloaded her suitcases from the trunk, then waited until she paid the fare. Alexis was shocked at the price but did not say so. *Welcome to the real world, Alex*, she thought ruefully.

"Have a good year, Miss," the cabby said warmly.

"Thanks." She smiled and stood alone on the sidewalk watching him drive away. She took a deep breath and walked up the steps and into the wide double doors. Once inside, she was awestruck by the hubbub of people and noise. Somehow, she managed to follow the signs and locate the registration desk. After standing in line for ten minutes, she was given a packet of information and numerous forms to fill out.

Weary from her travels, Alexis looked around for a place to sit down. Glad to be wearing pants, she followed what other students were doing and sat on a step of the wide staircase, unknowingly releasing a loud sigh.

"This is only the beginning," said a female voice from behind her.

Alexis turned around to face a pretty redheaded girl seated one step above her. The girl's eyes twinkled as she told Alexis, "Just be glad they aren't testing you on it!" Extending her hand, she said, "Hi, I'm Jenny."

"I'm Alex," she replied. "Are you new here, too?"

Jenny shook her head. "This is my third year. I only have to fill out a few forms. I shouldn't have any, but my paperwork got lost or something."

Alexis smiled, and patiently set about answering all of the questions on the papers. She did not understand why there were so many different forms; after all, her application had already been accepted.

After what seemed like forever, she had finished writing and laid down her pen. Only then did she realize that Jenny sat waiting for her. "All done? Just turn them back in to the registrar. He'll give you your room assignment."

Alexis smiled gratefully. While Jenny waited, the registrar took the papers from Alexis and gave her a card bearing a room number and location, as well as a meal ticket. After Jenny received her assignment as well, they walked outside together into the warm September day. It wasn't until that moment that Alexis realized her luggage was still sitting on the sidewalk!

They laughed together. "Which dorm are you in?" Jenny asked.

Alexis showed her the name on the card. "Do you know where that is?"

"Yes," Jenny pointed, "it's down there. But I'm going in the opposite direction. It was nice to meet you, Alex. Hope to see you around soon."

"You too," Alex told her sincerely. "Thanks for your help."

"I didn't do anything to help," Jenny laughed, "except maybe make your first impression a bit nicer, eh?"

Nodding, Alexis grabbed a bag in each hand and set off down the hill to locate her dorm. Upon reaching the building that was to be her home for the next nine months, she took the elevator to the third floor. She walked down the hall, studying the numbers on the doors until arriving at her own room. Unlocking the door, she stepped inside.

The drably painted two-room apartment was a sharp contrast to her bright, sunny yellow bedroom at Pender Harbor. Metal bunkbeds lined one wall, which also held a large armchair. Two identical desks sat by the window overlooking the shrubbery below. A large dresser and two matching bookshelves finished off the furnishings. To the right was a tiny bathroom and a closet with two separate compartments. The apartment looked comfortable enough, but, glancing around, Alexis felt a twinge of homesickness. A few posters would help. And plants. Or maybe her roommate would have some pretty pictures to hang. Frowning, Alexis wondered if she would have a roommate, and if so, would the two of them like each other? Having no sisters or brothers, Alexis sometimes felt she had missed out on certain social aspects of life.

She didn't have long to wait. Alexis had barely set her suitcases on the bed and unlocked the latch when the door opened.

"Hi!" came an excited voice behind her. "Are you my roommate?"

Alexis turned to greet the newcomer, a tall, gawky-looking young woman with long, straight brown hair, wearing blue jeans and a blouse and sensible shoes.

"Hi, I'm Alexis," she said shyly.

"And I'm Doris." When Doris smiled, Alexis felt warmed from head to toe. She would soon learn that what Doris lacked in poise and grooming she made up for in putting people at ease and showing interest in what others had to say. But for the moment, they stared at each other a bit awkwardly, then Doris said, "Well, you were here first--top or bottom?"

"What?" Alexis said dumbly.

Doris laughed. "Do you want the top or bottom bunk?"

"Oh! I'd probably fall off the top--may I have the bottom?"

"Sure. I like the top better anyway." Doris opened her suitcase and began pulling out clothes.

"Are you a first-year?" Alexis asked her.

"Sure am. How about you?"

Alexis laughed. "You mean you can't tell by just looking at me? I feel so unsure of myself. Like I've just stepped into another world or something."

Doris gave her a bright smile. "You have! The only reason I know anything at all about this place is because I took the 'royal tour' last spring when trying to figure out which college to go to."

"Was it a hard decision?"

"Not really. St. Mary's Regional Hospital also has a nursing program, but it's crammed so tight into two years that you don't even get time to breathe." She paused. "I'm in no hurry. I want to be a nurse, but I still want to be breathing when I get there!"

Having claimed their beds, they quickly agreed on who would use which desk and bookshelf. The two of them spent the next couple of hours unpacking and arranging their few chosen treasures from home. By early evening, their room had been transformed.

"Now all we need is some pictures," Doris said brightly. "Did you bring any?"

Alexis shook her head. She didn't mention the framed photograph of Cliff which she usually kept on her nightstand, for she was certain that wasn't the kind of picture Doris meant. "How about you?"

"No... but we can deal with that later. It's time to eat, and I'm absolutely starved. Shall we go?"

"Do you know where the cafeteria is?" Alexis asked.

"Sure. Come on. Don't forget your meal ticket."

In the hubbub of the lunchroom, Alexis was grateful to know at least one person. Students swarmed about, only a handful of whom seemed to know where to go and what to do. She did not see Jenny but there were so many students Jenny could have been a few feet away without her knowing.

Alexis was shocked at the abundance and selection of food in the buffet line. Several main dishes were offered, as well as numerous salads, breads, and desserts. Being so confined to the harbor most of the time, Alexis and her parents hardly ever ate a meal in town. Besides, her mother was an excellent cook so there had been no need. This would *definitely* take some getting used to!

Doris, too, seemed surprised. "Wow, school food has certainly taken a turn for the better," she murmured. "No wonder UBC costs so much!"

They found a table for two in the back of the large room, and Alexis was grateful to be alone with her roommate. She suddenly felt very tired and did not care to be thrown into the middle of a bunch of noisy students. She just wanted to get a good night's rest to be ready for her first day of classes tomorrow.

Doris, on the other hand, was a bundle of energy, chatting happily as she ate. She didn't seem to notice Alexis's lack of response, or the single tear that trickled down her roommate's cheek at the mention of Doris's parents. When the meal was over, they placed their dishes in the proper tubs and walked back to the room together.

That night as Alexis lay in bed, she stared at the metal slats in the bunk above her and let her thoughts wander. She could hear night noises in the distance, but not like those at Pender Harbor. Here the sounds were of other girls shuffling down the hall, doors closing and opening, a plane flying overhead, a car horn blaring. Alexis thought of the quiet sloshing of the water at the harbor, the humming of her mother going about her work, and her father's snoring as he snoozed in his easy chair.

She thought of the dark-haired, muscled boy that had so wildly captured her attention and wondered where he was at ten o'clock on that particular Tuesday evening. Probably lying on his own bed in his own dorm room at his own college, hundreds of miles away. Was he thinking about her at all? Would he ever think about her again?

Fighting tears, she rolled over and drifted into a restless sleep.

Studies soon absorbed all of Alexis's time and attention, and she had little time to be homesick OR to think about Cliff. As the weeks progressed, she found that she enjoyed the demands of college life. Learning was a joy, even though it meant hours sitting in class and then more hours studying. Her curiosity was insatiable, and, reminded of her father telling her to "look it up in the book," she scoured her textbooks for answers.

Alexis faithfully called or emailed home to let her parents know how things were going. After all, she reasoned, it was *their* money that was putting her through school. And they worked hard enough to earn it. She gave details about her teachers, her classes, and her friends. In return, her mother wrote notes now and then, and even sent a "care package" of goodies the first month.

She and Doris had purchased several inexpensive posters to cover their walls. The room still lacked the comfort of home, but that was to be expected, she supposed. Doris was a warm and caring roommate, sympathetic to her confessions of homesickness and always full of surprises. For the first dreaded exam, the two had stayed up late into the night studying and taking turns walking to the vending machine down the hall. The day she pulled Cliff's picture from her suitcase to set on her nightstand, she and Doris had stayed up late declaring their affections. Doris's own secret crush was a boy named Pete Swenson from her first period class.

Besides Doris she had made numerous other friends and never lacked for a ride to town when needed. The bus line was nearby and very convenient as long as she returned before service ended for the day. On Saturday nights a group of friends, always with Jenny, too, often left their studies behind for pizza or a movie. Before she knew it, the air had turned chilly, and the rains had come. Another month and she could go home for a visit.

"Are you going to the Thanksgiving banquet?" Doris asked her one afternoon after classes.

"Oh--well, I really hadn't given it much thought," Alexis responded. The banquet was fast approaching, and all of her classmates seemed to be going. "Do you have to have a date?"

"Oh, yeah--it is DEFINITELY a couples thing," Doris replied. "I'm told there's always really good music, usually a band of some sort, and the food is great."

Alexis groaned. "As if I need anything else to eat! I've already gained three pounds this semester! I can't imagine what I'd look like if I weren't walking so much every day!"

Doris smiled sympathetically. Her own slender figure had changed little. "Clinton asked me," she confided. "I haven't answered him yet, though--I'm kind of holding out for Pete!"

"Doris!" Alexis scolded, then laughed. "How fickle! No wonder women have such a reputation!"

Promptly forgetting about the banquet, Alexis kept busy studying for an upcoming biology test. With her nose buried in a book early one evening, she almost forgot to break for supper. Glancing up and noticing the time, she threw her book aside and ran a brush through her hair.

"Hey, Al!" came a voice from behind her as she walked up the long hill. It was Gary, a boy she shared lab assignment with. She half-scowled, half-grinned at the nickname he had given her.

"Hey, yourself! Are you headed to the dining hall?"

"Yeah. It's kinda late, but a guy has to eat. Speaking of which--" he hesitated. "I was wondering...."

He seemed ill at ease, and Alexis hoped nothing was wrong.

"I was wondering...if you're going to the banquet. I mean, would you like to go to the Thanksgiving banquet with me?" He stopped and blew air out his mouth as though he had just accomplished a great feat.

"Oh." Alexis stopped and stared at him.

"That is, if you're not, I mean--if you aren't already going with someone," he said, stumbling over his words.

She gave the idea some thought. Gary was an interesting lab partner, but she had not considered him in any way other than friend. Though she had tried to forget about Cliff, his picture on her bedside was a constant reminder. And in her mind, she had determined there would be no time for relationships if she wanted to graduate with high marks. Besides, she really didn't know Gary at all, except for being in the one class with him.

Gary was waiting, his blue eyes sparkling and his wavy blonde hair ruffling in the breeze as he stared down at her.

"Well?"

She laughed. "I'm sorry, Gary. You caught me totally by surprise. I hadn't even given the banquet much thought. Yes, it would be fun to go with you."

Instantly relieved, and obviously pleased, Gary let out a sigh. "Great. It's a week from tomorrow. I'll pick you up at your dorm." He turned to leave.

"Gary?"

"Yeah?"

"I thought you were going to supper!"

"Oh! Yeah!" He laughed. "Mind if I join you?"

"Not at all." She smiled over at him, feeling like she was leading him on. In her heart she still loved Cliff. But who knew what could happen? Maybe Gary would be so charming he would make her forget all about Cliff Hunter.

Maybe.

"Jenny, I don't have a thing to wear," Alexis complained to her friend the next day as they walked to the lunchroom together. She took a tray and selected a bowl of vegetable soup and a sandwich. Eyeing the choice of desserts, she picked up a large piece of lemon meringue pie, then sat down at a corner table.

"Let's go shopping!" Jenny suggested, setting her own tray on the table. "I know all the good places! Can you go tomorrow?"

"Yes, I suppose so. I should study for the biology exam, but--"

"Oh, come on, girl," Jenny chided. "I can see I'm going to have to help you have a little fun in your life!"

"Look who's talking!" Alexis laughed. "You won't even date!"

Jenny flashed a large diamond at her, pretending to smooth her hair. "That's because a certain man has a claim on me, if you'll recall," she said smugly. "And he promised to beat up anyone who came near me! Anyway, how about shopping?"

"Well...." Alexis hesitated. "I kind of hate to spend the money. Do you by chance have a dress I could borrow?"

Her friend took a bite of her sandwich and shook her head. "I didn't even bring any nice dresses, since I'm going home for all the holidays. But I know a dress shop that will have some good bargains. Besides, it'll be fun. Let's go tomorrow, okay? You can stay up late tonight to study."

Alexis felt her resistance weakening. "Okay," she grinned. "But I'd better stop eating, or I won't wear the same size in a week!" She frowned. "Want my pie?"

Jenny laughed.

By ten o'clock the next morning the girls were in the middle of busy downtown Vancouver. "Wow," Alexis breathed, overwhelmed. "I always forget how imposing it is. All these tall buildings!"

Jenny laughed.

"You have to understand," Alexis went on. "In Pender Harbor there's nothing higher than a sailboat helm!"

They examined rack after rack in the first shop but found nothing suitable. Even Jenny, for whom money was not an obstacle, was not impressed. "They usually have such good prices," she defended. "But these are expensive, and they're not even the least bit cute!"

Four stores later Alexis paused before a rack of gowns, and gasped. She held out a peach and cream floral print dress in a soft-flowing fabric for her friend to see. "Jenny, look! Isn't this beautiful! I bet it costs a fortune!"

"Ooooh." Jenny's eyes widened. She pulled out the price tag. "Nope, only forty dollars. Why don't you try it on?"

Alexis quickly found a dressing room and pulled off her shirt and pants. Slipping the smooth fabric over her head, she was pleased to note that the dress practically floated around her. With its lace-up detailing and accent at the waist, the dress was flattering to her figure as well as her complexion. She stepped outside the tiny room to get Jenny's opinion.

Jenny smiled. "That's definitely you," she agreed. "What do you think?"

Alexis nodded her head eagerly. "Think Gary will like it?"

"If he doesn't, the man is blind," Jenny answered solemnly.

When Gary rang the buzzer for her the following week, Alexis was just putting the finishing touches on her hair. Doris had already left for the evening, and her heart did a little flutter before leaving the room. This was her first date since Doug Pender earlier in the year. Was it only last summer? It seemed so long ago...her whole life had changed since then.

She took a deep breath and grabbed her purse. Just before opening the door, she noticed Cliff's dark brooding eyes staring at her from the framed photograph. Grinning, she blew him a kiss and left, closing the door behind her.

When the elevator doors opened, she saw Gary waiting for her in the lounge. His nervousness apparent, he walked back and forth in front of the sofa, a clear plastic florist's box in his right hand. Smiling, Alexis waited a few seconds until he looked over, then stepped out of the elevator and walked toward him. His face broke out into a relieved grin, and he held the box out to her.

"You look great," he said softly. "This is for you."

At least six foot five, with wavy blonde hair and blue eyes, Gary's good looks were not lost on Alexis. Though she hadn't really noticed him before, she had to admit that in his light blue shirt and navy sports jacket, he was strikingly handsome. Alexis smiled up at him as she accepted the peach-colored rose corsage from his hand.

"It's beautiful," she breathed. "Thank you." She flashed him a sincere smile, then asked, "Could you put it on for me?"

"I've never been very good at that," he began, "that's why I bought you a wrist corsage."

"Oh!" Alexis was delighted. Gingerly she removed the arrangement from the box and guided it over her left wrist. Slipping her arm through Gary's, she asked, "Shall we go?"

The meal was delicious, featuring chicken parmesan with rice pilaf, Caesar salad, cooked vegetable medley, rolls, and cheesecake for dessert. Gary's sense of humor made for a fun evening and entertained not only her but everyone at their table. The band was lively, with good music, but a little loud for Alexis's taste. She smiled as she noticed Doris across the room, evidently laughing at something Clinton had said. To Doris's disappointment, Pete Swenson had chosen someone else for his date.

Since the dinner had been held at a restaurant near the Washington state border, Gary asked Alexis upon leaving the parking lot whether she had ever been in the United States.

She shook her head. "No reason to. Remember, I've been pretty tied down to the harbor all my life."

"Lady, you haven't lived!" he said jokingly. "I'm going to make this an evening you won't forget!"

Before Alexis could protest, he was on the highway headed in the opposite direction from where they had come.

"Gary! Where are you taking me?" she protested, for the moment wishing they had doubled with another couple.

"Little lady," he drawled in his best imitation of John Wayne, "I'm takin' you for a ride. Do you have your enhanced driver's license?"

"Yes!" she practically shouted, and squealed, attempting to object and being playfully stopped by her escort. Almost before she knew it, the car was entering Peace Arch Park in line behind others, and soon pulled up alongside the border station.

"And where are you two headed tonight?" asked the solemn border patrolman from his narrow window.

"This lady has never been in the United States before," said Gary honestly, "and I think it's high time."

The patrolman seemed to hesitate, then asked, "Are you carrying any fruit?"

"No, sir."

"How long will you be?"

"Actually, we'll be back within an hour," Gary replied seriously.

"Go ahead," the patrolman told them after checking their IDs, the hint of a smile playing at his lips.

When they had pulled safely away and out of sight, Alexis burst out laughing. "The guy looked so serious for a minute there, I thought he was going to search the car!"

"They do, sometimes," Gary told her. "For no reason at all except maybe somebody looks suspicious or seems to be up to no good." He pulled the car into a parking spot nearby. "Wanna walk?"

Alexis shrugged. "Sure! I've never walked on U.S. soil before! Does it feel the same?"

Gary opened the passenger door and took her hand, guiding her from the car. Getting more in the spirit every minute, Alexis took off her high-heeled pumps and carried them in her hand while they walked side by side across the soft grass. A full moon allowed them plenty of light for their stroll.

The evening was chilly, and Alexis was glad she had worn a light jacket over her dress. "This is really nice, Gary," she said appreciatively.

"It is, isn't it?" He smiled at her. "Especially when you're in good company."

Writing home to her parents the following week, Alexis could only smile about her evening with Gary. "He's not a thing like Cliff," she wrote, "or Doug either.

49

But I like him. And he's so FUNNY! At least if I don't fall in love with him, he could keep me laughing so hard I'd forget about Cliff!!"

Sticking to her studies, Alexis was pleasantly surprised to receive very high marks on her mid-term exams. Proudly she mailed the reports home to her parents, penciling in, "See, Daddy, all those fish bellies I cut open *did* do some good!" She could imagine her father's face, with the smile she so loved, as he read her words.

"Alexis, I've been thinking," Jenny began one day as they carried their lunch trays to a table. "Would you like to go home with me for Thanksgiving?"

Alexis's mouth dropped open. "To Grouse Mountain?" Jenny's parents owned a lodge there.

Jenny nodded, setting down her tray and taking a sip of water. "It would be so much fun! Have you ever been on the cable car before? Do you ski?"

"No--to both questions. And it sounds like fun! A lot of fun...." She hesitated. "It's just that.... Have you already asked your mom and dad?" The trip in itself sounded like an adventure, but Alexis was torn. She was so looking forward to seeing her parents.

"Yes, and they'd love to have you! What do you think?" Jenny's bright eyes pleaded.

After much consideration as well as a phone call home, Alexis decided to go. After all, she reasoned, she would see her parents at Christmas, and when would she get a chance like this again? Excited, she and Jenny discussed their plans. Alexis planned to pack as lightly as possible, since the trip was only for a few days. And the cable car up the mountain was the only way to get there.

Cable car. The thought both excited and frightened Alexis. She had never been up that high before; the truth was, she had a feeling she'd feel a lot safer alone on a boat at six in the morning!

When that weekend finally arrived, Jenny came for her promptly at seven. "You ready?" she asked, whisking into the room like a fresh breeze. Her freckled nose was red from the already-cold weather, her eyes shining with excitement. "Don't forget your boots and gloves!"

They were out the door within minutes. As Jenny's little car sped through town, Alexis had to remind her of the speed limit. Jenny giggled.

"I'm so excited. My family's just going to love you--I've told them all about you. And you're going to *love* Fred! He'll be so happy to meet you!"

Alexis's eyes twinkled. "Yeah, right--like Fred will even *notice* me with his fiancée home, you nut!"

Jenny's laughter filled the car. Before they knew it, they were on the ferry. The two girls could hardly contain their excitement and chattered all the way. Nearing the other side, they hurried back down the stairs to the car. When their turn came, they drove off the ferry and were quickly on their way again.

The moment had arrived. Alexis held her breath as she stepped onto the cable car. It felt secure enough while it was on the platform, but within minutes they would be dangling above the trees. The other guests were bustling with excitement and Alexis tried to hide her own nervousness.

"Well?" Jenny asked moments later when the trip had begun.

Alexis only raised her eyebrows.

Later on, she had to admit that it was the most adventurous thing she had ever done in her life. It was a little frightening to be dangling so far above the ground, and since she had never ridden a plane, it was the highest she had ever been.

The second most adventurous thing was her first attempt at skiing. On borrowed skis, Alexis placed one foot at a time down onto the snowy slope and tried to slide a little each time.

"You're getting the hang of it!" encouraged Fred. Jenny was right, Alexis *did* just "love" Jenny's fiancé. At least, she could certainly understand why Jenny did. He was a warm, caring young man, a gentleman, and his physical attributes were nothing to scoff at.

"If you two weren't engaged, I'd fall for him myself!" she teased Jenny one evening as they undressed for bed. Jenny made a face and threw a pillow at her.

The short vacation was over all too soon, and the girls returned to school. The weeks between

Thanksgiving and Christmas flew by. Before she knew it, Alexis was on the ferry headed home. As the horn blared just before pulling into Langdale, Alexis spotted her mother and father waiting for her. She waved frantically, and, their faces brightening, they waved back.

"Oh Mom, Dad, it's so good to see you!" She gave them both a hug and they all three tried to talk at once. Her father, usually the more talkative of the three, kept shutting his mouth so not to interrupt his wife. Her mother seemed bursting with news.

"We've missed you so!" from Kate.

"The house has been kinda quiet," from her father.

"Your old high school group is getting together on Friday," Kate told her. "Doug called to see if you would be home."

"You're kidding! Doug called me?" Alexis was shocked. Then, quietly, she asked her mother, "Any word from Cliff?"

"We got a Christmas card from him," her mother responded. "No note, just his signature. I'm sorry, dear."

Her father loaded her suitcase in the trunk, and they drove away from the dock and headed home. Alexis fell suddenly quiet. She had so hoped to hear something from Cliff. Being home made her think of how things used to be...when Cliff was around....

Alexis was grateful her parents had waited for her arrival so they could decorate the tree together. They spent a contented evening hanging ornaments and balls and stringing a popcorn chain. Her father groaned as Alexis insisted on stringing the tinsel. "I never could stand the stuff," he muttered.

She only laughed.

On Friday the old high school group met for pizza and bowling. Doug Pender had insisted on picking her up, warning her of snowy roads. He stayed close to her all evening, then suggested they stop for coffee on the way home. Doug seemed as eager to hear her news of college life as he was to share his own. Conversation came easily with him, and she was glad that he still considered her a friend.

After the welcome two-week stay was over, Alexis was back at college again hitting the books. That semester sped by, and before she knew it there was only one month to go before summer. By now she had packed away the picture of Cliff, as Gary was asking her out more and more all the time. She refused him often, pleading she was busy with homework. The truth was, she wanted no commitments but was afraid of hurting his tender feelings. In her heart she was still holding out hope for Cliff but wanted to be realistic, too. It was very possible that she would never again hear from Cliff Hunter. Even so, though Gary was nice, Alexis was only interested in him as a friend.

Finding it difficult to concentrate since the arrival of spring, Alexis lay sprawled on her bed studying one warm May evening when her phone's ring tone interrupted her thoughts. Her mother's ID showed on the face, which was unusual since her mother was usually making dinner about this time of day.

"Honey, it's Mom." Her mother's voice sounded wobbly and far away.

"Mom--hi! Is everything okay? You sound--"

"No, honey, it's not. I need you to come home right away." Her voice broke. "It's your dad. He had a heart attack."

Alexis's heart skipped a beat. "Is he--is he going to be all right?"

The silence on the other end gripped her heart with fear.

"Mom, where is he?"

"At St. Mary's, in Sechelt."

"Okay--I'm on my way." She glanced at her watch. "I'll have to hurry to catch the last ferry. That should put me into Sechelt around eleven-thirty."

"Okay, sweetie. I'll see you when you get here. And Alexis--pray!" Her mother's voice sounded urgent.

Alexis spoke to God with a fervor she had never known before. "Please, God, please, let my dad be okay." She began pulling open drawers, packing her jeans and shirts, then threw in her make-up bag and toothbrush. Her mind raced--who to call first, what to do next. She had no idea where Doris was, but hopefully Jenny could give her a ride to the terminal. She plugged in her number.

"Jenny, this is Alex. Listen, I need a ride to the ferry terminal right away. My dad had a heart attack. Can you take me?"

Without hesitation, Jenny replied, "I'll be right over."

While she waited for Jenny, she called Gary to let him know what was going on.

Gary's voice was caring. "I'm so sorry, Al. I hope everything works out okay. Take care--call me, and let me know how he's doing, huh?"

She blinked back tears and nodded, then realized he couldn't hear her nod through the phone and said, "Okay." Gary would have given her a ride, she knew, but he was an off-campus student and lived across town with his parents.

There was a quick rap at the door before it burst open. It was Jenny, her bright blue eyes eager. "You ready?"

"Yes. I just have to leave a note for my roommate." Alexis scribbled on a loose piece of paper and placed it on Doris's bed. As an afterthought, she grabbed a couple of dresses from the closet along with her jacket. She had no idea how long she would be gone or what she would need.

Alexis had not considered how to get from the Sechelt terminal to the hospital, and when Jenny offered to go along for the entire trip, she was more than grateful. Boarding the ferry, they left the car and found a secluded table near the food stands. The ferry carried only a handful of people so late in the evening, and the forty-five-minute ride seemed endless.

"My dad could be dying," Alexis lamented. "And we're stuck on this--this tank! I wish I had the Seaswirl."

Jenny smiled sympathetically.

At last, they reached Langdale. Jenny's small car sped over the dark winding roads as Alexis told her where to go. When they pulled into the hospital parking lot near midnight, Jenny parked the car in the first empty spot available and they ran inside.

"Charlie--Charles Ryan," Alexis told the woman behind the desk, "he--" She broke into tears.

"He had a heart attack," Jenny calmly explained. "Can you tell us what room he's in? This is his daughter, Alexis."

Alexis nodded. The receptionist, while seemingly sympathetic, would tell them very little. Mr. Ryan had been admitted to the hospital earlier that evening, she said as she checked her charts, then taken from his room for some tests. She asked the girls to have a seat while she called the nurse's station on his floor.

A panic-stricken glance passed between the girls. "But at least that means he's alive," Alexis said brightly. "I wonder where my mom is."

Just then the elevator doors opened, and Mrs. Ryan rushed down the hall. "Oh, honey, I'm so glad you're here!" She gave her daughter a quick hug.

"Mom--how's Dad?"

"He's okay, sweetie, he really is. He's sleeping now. But the doctor says he won't be able to keep up the same pace after this. He'll need straight bed rest for a while, then a slower lifestyle. And you know how your dad is."

Alexis was quiet as she took in what her mother was saying. Then, relieved, she began to cry, and they hugged each other again.

"Oh--" Alexis realized she had not introduced her guest. "Mom, this is my friend Jenny, the one who lives at Grouse Mountain. She gave me a ride."

"I'm so grateful to you, Jenny. Now let's go home, girls. Jenny, you're staying the night, aren't you?"

Jenny nodded.

Kate's ash-blonde hair looked gray, and her face was weary and drawn. She turned tired eyes to Alexis. "Your dad's sedated and won't be awake until morning. There's nothing we can do. If there's a change, they'll call us."

Alexis rode with Kate while Jenny followed in her own car. She pumped her mother with questions on the half-hour drive home. Kate filled her in as best she could, then yawned.

"I'm so tired, Alexis," she told her daughter, then said, "I'm so glad you're home--we've missed you. Your father will feel better just seeing you."

The comment warmed Alexis's heart. She had missed her parents, too. Her mother would need her help now more than ever before.

A sudden realization came to Alexis: she would not be returning to college, not even for the last month of the semester. With Charlie convalescing, Kate would have her hands full. Her parents needed her at home. *Now.*

Alexis confided this to Jenny later on, lying on the bed in the darkness. Jenny was quiet, then asked, "Will you be back to collect your things?"

"I think so. Maybe in a week or two. I'll talk to Mom in the morning. It's too early yet to tell what will happen."

They left for the hospital early the next day. Upon entering her father's room, Alexis found him sitting up in bed and watching the news on television. Rushing to his bedside, Kate gave him a gentle kiss and the two shared a private look of understanding. Alexis politely waited, then embraced him in a warm hug.

"Well, you gave us quite a scare," she told him. "How are you feeling?"

In the blue hospital garb her father looked very little like the gruff fisherman everyone knew. With his hair uncombed, his face wore a tired, haggard look, his expression drawn. But the twinkle in his eyes as he answered told Alexis his sense of humor had returned.

"I feel ornery," Charlie admitted. "Like I could eat somebody." Noticing the timid figure standing behind Alexis, he softened, addressing the stranger. "But don't worry, young lady, I won't."

Alexis laughed. "Dad, this is Jenny. She drove me from college and spent the night."

"Pleased to meet you, Jenny. Tell me, are all Alexis's friends so pretty?"

The red-haired girl stood blushing. With her bright blue eyes and red hair, Jenny had attracted the eye of many a medical student during the past several months, though she ignored them all. Alexis and her mother glanced at each other and burst out laughing. They knew Charlie was going to be okay.

Just before Jenny left later that day, Alexis took her for a short boat ride down the inlet. Jenny was thrilled at the beauty all around. She shivered, hugging her down jacket closer to her body, and sighed. "Wow, Alexis, you grew up with this?"

Alexis nodded. "This is my life. Quite different from yours, huh?" She paused. "Cliff and I spent many hours in this boat. More than I can remember." Alexis had long-ago confided her well-kept secret.

Jenny laid a hand on her friend's arm. "Listen, Alex, Cliff may not be in the picture anymore. But I know someone who is. Or at least, *wants* to be."

Grateful for the reminder, Alexis called Gary that evening at his home. Though he was glad for the encouraging news of her father's prognosis, his voice was filled with disappointment that Alexis would not be returning to school. She and her mother had talked it over, and, sadly, her mother agreed it was for the best.

"But--what about all your stuff?" he asked her. "Want me to bring it to you?"

She smiled, grateful that she had a friend as thoughtful as Gary. "Oh, Gary, that's sweet--but next week I plan to come pack up my stuff and say all my goodbyes. Thanks for the offer."

As promised, the following week she made a quick trip back to college to collect her things, staying only one more night in the dorm room with Doris. She said tearful goodbyes to her classmates, vowing to return when she could. Jenny promised to visit again sometime, but knowing Jenny was getting married that summer and starting a whole new life, Alexis doubted they would see each other for a long time. Gary said with a long face that he would miss her and gave her a brotherly hug. Alexis tactfully discouraged him from visiting her in Pender Harbor, thanked him for his friendship, and wished him the best for whatever his future held.

At the dorm she loaded her baggage into the trunk of the car, hugged Doris, and drove quickly away.

* * *

Chapter Five

Life in the harbor took on its usual routine once again, except for Charlie not being around to banter with the guests or guide boats into the water. As the regular customers began arriving, they asked about him, and the house soon became filled with bedside visitors. Still feeling he was missing out on the activities, though, Charlie set up camp in a lounge chair on the deck of the big house where he could see what was going on.

The two women joked about him. "Well, I guess he's doing *his* job," said Kate. "Sometimes I think he's the only reason people come back after their first visit. He always makes them feel as though he's known them for years."

Alexis smiled. Yes, her father truly had that gift. The "gift of gab" he was fond of saying, but Alexis knew it was more than that. Her mother being the less talkative of the two, she preferred a quiet conversation with a close friend. Charlie, on the other hand, thrived on meeting new people, showing them around, and helping them in whatever way he could. He would *definitely* not have been happy with a desk job. His special qualities made him a natural at running the harbor.

After helping her mother for the next few weeks, Alexis was worn out. When June arrived, she was glad for the summer staff to arrive as well. No more maid service for her. She gladly took her former position of tending the counter and showing guests to their rooms.

Scanning the guest book one afternoon, Alexis smiled. Life seemed back to normal--her father was recuperating nicely, she had her old job back, Kate was in the kitchen baking, and all the guest rooms were full. She only wished she could have finished nursing school. *No regrets*, she chided herself. *You're needed here now. They were always here for you. It's your turn to do something for them.* She lifted a diet soda out of the cooler and pulled the tab.

Noticing a dark blue Blazer drive up outside the office, Alexis was prepared to tell its occupant they were booked up, that they would have to go down the road to the next resort. Double-checking the reservations, her head was lowered over the registration book when the office door opened, and a tall, dark-haired, good-looking man strode over to the counter.

Cliff stood before her. She could feel his warm gaze even before looking up. Their eyes met. His were darker, his face fuller, and he was even more handsome than Alexis remembered. Her mouth dropped open in surprise.

"Alex," he said simply, with an unreadable expression on his face, "I'm back."

Alexis burst out crying, and Cliff walked around behind the counter to take her in his arms.

"I know I'm taking a lot for granted," he murmured into her hair, "so stop me any time you want to."

Far from resisting, Alexis buried her face in his chest and let the tears flow. All of the emotions of the last year spilled out. "Oh, Cliff, it's just that--it's just that we need you. My dad--"

"I know, honey, I know. It's okay. Everything's going to be okay."

Alexis blinked. Had he just called her 'honey'?

Cliff brushed her tears away and kissed her soundly on the lips. Both were too preoccupied to notice guests walking by and glancing curiously in the window.

"How did you find out about Dad?" Alexis asked after Cliff had wiped her tears away. Cliff sat on the edge of the counter, his long legs dangling, and Alexis stood facing him.

"I called you a couple weeks ago," Cliff replied.

"You did? But how--"

"Your parents gave me the number a while back when I asked for it. I couldn't decide whether to call you or not, and when I finally did you didn't answer."

Alexis frowned. "That's funny...my parents didn't say anything about you calling."

Cliff went on. "I called the school to leave you a message, and the person at the front desk told me you had gone home because of a family emergency. When I told her who I was and pressed her for information, she told me what had happened. She seemed to already *know* who I was."

He paused while Alexis tried not to smile. Of *course,* the receptionist--none other than Doris--knew who he was. She and Doris had only stayed up late talking about him more nights than she could count. She had kept his picture on her nightstand only a few months. After she started dating Gary, she had placed the beloved photograph carefully back into her suitcase.

"After that I just decided to come in person," he continued. A twinkle came into his eyes. "Is my old job still available?"

"Is that why you came back?" Alexis asked, trying not to get her hopes up.

"What do you think?" he said softly. He pulled her into his arms and gave her a long, passionate kiss that sent her pulse racing.

"I think if we're going to keep this up, we'd better go where everyone's not walking by and staring at us!" Alexis admitted, laughing as someone opened the office door. "Why don't you go on up to the house. Mom and Dad will be so surprised! I'll come when I'm done here," she said, turning to her smiling customer. Cliff reluctantly left, flashing her a wink as he exited.

Entering the front door a couple of hours later, she found Cliff engaged in lively conversation with her father.

"Were they surprised?" Alexis asked Cliff.

"Yes, but they sure didn't give me as warm a welcome as *you* did!" Cliff answered mischievously. Blushing, she excused herself to the kitchen to help her mother with dinner.

"What have we here? Chocolate cake?" Alexis teased. "For me?"

Kate smiled. "You know it's Cliff's favorite. He sweet-talked me into making layered salad and hush puppies, too."

Alexis whistled. It appeared that Cliff's charms worked on her mother as well.

"I can't believe he's here! Mom, why didn't you tell me Cliff called?" Alexis asked. "He said he got the number from you."

"I didn't want to get your hopes up, honey," Kate admitted. "I figured if he called, I wouldn't need to say anything. And if he didn't, then you wouldn't be heartbroken because you wouldn't have known he was going to."

Thinking it over, Alexis was touched. "Thanks Mom," she said, impulsively giving her mother a hug. "You're a wise lady, ya know?"

"I'm a mother," Kate said simply, and began stirring the batter for the hush puppies. Alexis chopped lettuce for salad and put the salmon in the oven to bake, then placed plates and cutlery on the quilted placemats. Cliff turned to smile at her as she set the table. She could hardly keep her eyes off him as he sat talking to her father. Was he really here?

As the four of them sat around the table that evening, Charlie looked more rested than he had in weeks, and Kate beamed. "Would you like to say grace, Cliff?" Kate asked, and Cliff reached over for Alexis's hand.

As Alexis listened to Cliff's deep voice thanking God for the food, for Charlie's good health, and for bringing Alexis back into his life, a chill went down her spine. So, he hadn't forgotten all about her after all! After his "Amen" the two stole a glance at each other and he squeezed her hand before releasing it.

During the meal Cliff filled them in on the latest activities of his life, and Alexis found herself mesmerized by his voice. How long had it been...? Two years since she had heard that voice. Two long years.

"Last fall my uncle died," Cliff was saying. "So, my aunt sold the house and moved to a smaller place. Before graduation I put in a ton of job applications all over Alaska--but I couldn't get my old job--or, Alex-- out of my mind." He reached over and clasped her hand again.

Alexis could hardly contain her excitement. She smiled at him, then stole a look at her mother, who appeared very pleased.

"Well," Cliff went on, laying down his fork and glancing over at Charlie. "Charlie, mind if I borrow the Seaswirl this evening to take your daughter for a ride? I promise to have her home on time." He grinned at Alexis and winked.

"Well, son, you'll have to talk to my daughter about the Seaswirl," Charlie drawled. "I bought a new Bayliner last year."

Cliff looked over at Alexis in surprise.

Alexis nodded. "Dad felt he had to keep up with all of his seafaring friends!"

"Oh, now, go on with you," Charlie waved a hand at her. "I don't have to keep up with anybody. It's just that--" The rest of his words were drowned out by the laughter around the table. Charlie lifted his hands in mock despair.

Cliff turned to Alexis. "Shall we go?" To Kate he said, "Kate, thank you for a wonderful dinner. I haven't had cooking like this for a long time!"

Alexis began to clear the table, but Kate motioned her to go. "I'll get this, honey," she told her daughter. "You go and have a good time."

"Thanks, Mom," she whispered.

The minute they were outside, Cliff pulled her to him in a tight embrace, his lips leaving a sweet chocolatey taste on her own.

"It's so good to see you again," he murmured, then drew back and looked her up and down. "How long has it been?"

"Two years," she told him solemnly. "Technically, only about one year, eight months, three weeks, and four days. But who's counting?"

Cliff sobered, then kissed her again and took her hand. "Did you think about me?" he asked as they walked down the hill to the dock.

"Only when I wasn't thinking about more exciting things, like lumbar vertebrae or latissimus dorsi," she teased. "Which was most of the time!"

They climbed into the boat and Alexis untied the rope. Cliff guided the boat skillfully onto the water, then cut the engine when they were far away from the harbor lights. Alone in the darkness, they climbed up onto the open bough and sat side by side, dangling their feet lazily over the edge of the boat. Alexis leaned over against Cliff. Wasn't this the moment she had dreamed of all her life? She could feel the rise and fall of his chest as he breathed, his heartbeat making a tiny thump against her ear. She thought she could stay there forever. There was so much they needed to say, yet words seemed unnecessary. For now, she thrilled at the nearness of him, at the earthy, musky scent of his skin and the tickle of his hair on her cheek.

"I've wanted to take you in my arms for years," Cliff said softly, nuzzling her hair with his lips.

Alexis was shocked at his confession. "Why didn't you?" she asked.

"I was waiting for you to grow up," he admitted. "Then I started dating a girl at school. And I wanted to give you time to know your own heart." He paused. "I tried to forget about you, but God wouldn't let me."

"That's because I was praying He wouldn't," she whispered. Her heart pounded in her chest. She turned slightly, as did Cliff, and their lips met in a hungry kiss.

"Alex, I've waited so long for this," he said huskily.

"Me, too," she whispered.

"Alex--"

"Yes, Cliff." She could barely see his face in the moonlight. His dark eyes were serious.

"I love you, Alex. Will you marry me?"

Her heart leapt. "Oh, Cliff, yes!"

They sealed the promise with another kiss, an even longer one. He hugged her tightly, then they laughed because it wasn't the safest thing to do on the bough of a boat, as the sloshing of the water rocked them gently back and forth.

"I've loved you since I was fifteen years old," she told Cliff soberly. "I was just waiting for you stop thinking of me as a kid and love me back. But since you didn't write, I figured you'd forgotten all about me. Then when you wrote that letter to my parents last summer, I thought you were never coming back."

"But I am back. I'm here, and I'm never going away again." Cliff pulled her tighter to him, and she sighed against his chest.

Not until well after midnight, as the two of them walked slowly hand in hand up the hill to the big house, did Alexis remember that all the units were booked! She giggled.

"What's so funny? Have you broken curfew again?"

"I forgot to tell you--all the rooms are full! You'll have to sleep on our couch, I guess, since we don't have an extra room anywhere on the place!"

"For how long?" Cliff asked.

Alexis was puzzled. "What do you mean, 'how long'? For tonight, silly. And probably tomorrow night. Then most of the weekenders will go home."

"No." He stopped in his tracks and pulled her to him. "For how long? How long do I have to stay away from you?"

Alexis blushed, just realizing his meaning. "Cliff, you're embarrassing me."

"Honey, all I'm trying to say is--WHEN will you marry me? I've already waited a long time."

"Soon," she whispered, her own desire rising within her. She was grateful Cliff held the same standards as she did, and they would wait for certain intimacies until their wedding night. She kissed him quickly, holding his cheeks between her hands for a moment and memorizing his face. "Very soon. Now let's go tell Mom and Dad the news."

This was one occasion, Alexis felt certain, for which they would want to be awakened. Surprisingly, her mother was still awake. As Cliff and Alexis walked through the front door, Kate glanced up from her paperwork. Alexis ran over and hugged her. "Mom-- guess what! Cliff asked me to marry him! And I said 'yes'!"

A full smile broke out on her mother's face as Cliff bent down to kiss her cheek. "Oh honey, I'm so happy. And Cliff dear--welcome to the family. You know we already love you like a son."

"Can I wake Daddy?" Alexis asked.

Kate hesitated. "Just this once."

Alexis walked quietly down the hall. When she heard her father's loud snoring, she didn't have the heart to disturb him. He had not slept so soundly since before his hospital stay. Idleness allowed him rest, but also made him restless at night from inactivity. Closing the door behind her, she let him sleep, making her mother promise to let the two of them give him the news in the morning.

"Oh, and Mom--" Alexis briefly explained to her mother about the sleeping situation. Kate laughed and went to get him a pillow. Cliff grabbed his sleeping bag from the Blazer and threw it onto the couch.

"Good night, ladies," he told them both. He hugged Kate, then walked over to Alexis after her mother had left the room.

"Sleep well, love," he said softly, and left a long, memorable kiss on her lips that set her heart racing.

* * *

Chapter Six

The next morning the family awoke later than usual. Alexis, for once the first to rise, went out to see if Cliff was up so they could talk to her dad together. Cliff lay asleep on the couch, his dark hair loose on the pillow. Alexis walked over and stood watching him for a few minutes. After reconsidering, she made a pot of coffee, then went back into the living room.

By this time Cliff had awakened and gave her a lazy smile. "Will you be the first thing I see every morning when we're married?" he asked her, pulling her down for a hug.

"I hope so," she admitted. "I can't believe last night really happened, can you? I thought maybe I dreamt you!"

"Not a chance," he said huskily.

Suddenly Kate cleared her throat from the doorway, and announced, "Alexis, your father's awake if you want to speak to him."

Her eyes widened and she stood up. "You didn't say anything, did you Mom?"

Kate smiled and shook her head. "Not a peep."

"Come on, sleepyhead," she told Cliff, pulling on his hand.

"What a nag!" he told Kate, laughing. "Is she always like this? You know," he told Alexis, "I can't get up with you standing there."

"What?"

"Alexis," Kate explained, "Let's go out to the kitchen and get your dad a cup of coffee. Cliff needs to put some clothes on."

Only then did Alexis notice his jeans flung over the armchair. "Oh!" She giggled. "Okay, but hurry," she told him.

Cliff appeared in the kitchen a few minutes later and they walked down the hall carrying a cup of coffee for Charlie. "Daddy, are you awake?" Alexis called out. "Can I come in?"

"Sure, honey," came the answer.

Charlie was sitting up in bed reading his Bible. Since his heart attack, his practice was to stay in bed until around ten, then go outside to his lounge chair on the deck. When he saw them both, his eyes widened. "If I'd known we were having an open house I would have dressed up," he told them with a grin.

"Daddy--I have something to tell you." Alexis fairly burst with the news. "Cliff has asked me to marry him!"

Charlie let out a loud "Whoop!" surprising them all. The sudden outburst brought Kate into the room, carrying a tray with oatmeal and toast for her husband.

"Does that mean you're happy for us?" Alexis asked.

"Honey, you don't know how I've prayed for this," her father admitted in a rare serious moment. "Not only for you, but--ya know, I'm not as young as I used to be. I was kinda hoping for a guy like Cliff to take over so I can retire."

Alexis's mouth dropped open.

"Cliff, we'll talk later," Charlie continued. "Think about what I've said. But son--I couldn't ask for a better man to fill my shoes...or to marry my daughter. I'm proud to have you in our family."

Cliff beamed. Alexis impulsively gave her dad a big hug. "Oh daddy, I love you."

Kate brushed back a tear. "I hadn't thought of that. Your dad's changed to a slower pace since his heart attack, but he still tries to do too much himself. Cliff, would you consider running the resort?"

He and Alexis exchanged glances. "I'd have to talk it over with my bride," he said quietly. "Can I let you know?"

After the couple prayed about it together and talked it over, the matter was soon decided. Alexis was thrilled that she wouldn't have to leave the harbor. She *did*, however, want a place to call their own. Given a choice between one of the mobile homes or a cottage, the couple settled on what had always been Alexis's favorite: a cozy two-bedroom A-frame cabin set in a cluster of trees near the water. The cabin would give them plenty of privacy while still being within sight of the office and her parents' home. She and Kate excitedly talked over decorating plans for the little cottage.

A week after his proposal, Cliff took Alexis fishing, as he had done so many times before. After both lines were in the water, he smiled over at her. "Just think, this is where it all started," he said, grinning.

"Sounds kinda fishy to me," Alexis quipped.

"Alex, do you have any joy plugs?" Cliff suddenly asked. He often used them in fishing but usually brought his own.

"Sure. Do you need one?"

He nodded. "Please."

She fumbled with her tackle box, the same pink one Cliff had given her on her sixteenth birthday. Pulling open the tiny plastic case containing several of the items he requested, she gasped. Lying in the bottom of the compartment was a diamond ring!

"Oh, Cliff! It's beautiful!"

Cliff's face wore a smug, satisfied look. "You like it?"

"Oh, I absolutely love it!" She held it up in the sunlight, watching the diamond sparkle as she moved it back and forth. "It's even prettier than Jenny's!"

"Try it on," he urged.

The ring, a diamond with tiny pearls on either side, fit perfectly.

Alexis was dumbfounded. "You sneak! And anyway, how did you know my size?"

"Your mom. We were hoping it was the same size as your class ring. Didn't figure your hand could get too much bigger in a year!"

Setting her pole securely in the holder, Alexis moved to sit next to Cliff in the boat, wrapping her arms tightly around him. Their lines dangled unnoticed in the water as they huddled close and shared plans, ideas, and hopes for their future together. They agreed on a September wedding at the harbor's community church where Alexis and her folks attended. Alexis would ask Jenny to be her maid of honor. Matron, she corrected herself, for Jenny's own wedding was just a month away. Hopefully Cliff's closest friend from boyhood days could drive up from Washington State to be his best man.

As harbor guests heard of the news, they congratulated Alexis and Cliff heartily. Many of them still remembered the skinny, white-chested boy and the girl in the dirty yellow T-shirt, and marveled that the two were finally getting together.

The summer sped by, with Alexis and her mother busily planning the many details for a fall wedding. At first Alexis consulted Cliff, but he gave his bride-to-be full rein for all wedding plans, claiming the only part of the wedding he wanted to be a part of was saying "I do" and kissing the bride. Besides that, he told her, Charlie was keeping him busier than ever before, training him on management responsibilities as well as maintenance. The only thing Cliff insisted on was that he *not* wear a white tuxedo and that Alexis not wear a veil. Laughing, Alexis decided to leave Cliff to his work and discuss the particulars with her mother.

Alexis took on more of Kate's responsibilities than ever before, giving her mother time to sew an old-fashioned satin dress with covered buttons. After several shopping trips, Alexis had been about to give up hope of finding the perfect dress in which to be married. When she discovered the beautiful, button-up-the-back gown in a mail-order catalog, the huge price listed underneath drove her to tears. Kate, coming to the rescue, said that she had sewn her own wedding dress, so why didn't she just make Alexis's as well? Alexis marveled at her mother's many talents and jumped in where she could to give her mother time to sew.

Since the little cabin that would soon be hers was solidly booked throughout the summer, Alexis anxiously waited until its last occupant drove away. She had taken full advantage of cleaning up between guests to note the colors, room sizes, and furniture. Now, with only two weeks before the wedding, Alexis began spending every spare moment there creating a home for her and Cliff. Faded paisley curtains were soon replaced with bright, cheery ones, and seashell wallpaper added to the bathroom would allow her to decorate with her favorite shells later on. Painting was unnecessary, but the carpet needed a good shampooing and the appliances hadn't been thoroughly cleaned in a long while. Alexis worked joyfully, humming as she worked, distracted only by the birds chirping outside the window. By now the dress was finished and her mother had released Alexis from her other duties. Two more weeks, and she would be Mrs. Cliff Hunter.

"Honey," Kate said to her one afternoon as Alexis was folding laundry, "will you go down to the cabin and bring me the coffeepot that's there? I need to borrow it for one of the other units."

Alexis, wondering which unit had a broken coffeepot, dutifully walked over to the cabin to retrieve the item. No sooner had she put the key in the lock and swung the door open than she heard a chorus of voices yell "Surprise!"

Startled, she gasped. There, crowded in the tiny kitchen and overflowing into the living room, were about thirty friends and guests, as well as her father. The little round table was laden with gifts, and the requested coffeepot sat innocently brewing fresh coffee. A large glass bowl of punch sat on the counter next to a colorfully decorated cake. Cliff stood grinning sheepishly at her from the sidelines. Kate appeared through the door a minute later, grinning from ear to ear.

"Oh! My! I--" Alexis sputtered, then burst out laughing and ran for the shelter of Cliff's arms. Everyone clapped, and the festivities began.

Alexis asked Cliff to write down each gift and its giver, for writing thank-you notes later on. At the moment, she was overwhelmed, not only with all of the guests and gifts but also at the well-kept surprise. Opening the packages one by one, she squealed after unwrapping a set of fluffy bathroom towels in seashell motif. Cliff seemed to enjoy being at his first-ever bridal shower, and bantered with the guests as each present was opened.

Kate disappeared several times to answer the office's buzzer, as she had penciled a large sign to "ring bell for service". Any new guests just checking in were invited over to the cabin for cake and punch.

After an hour of gift opening, Alexis sat surrounded by new pots and pans, a beautiful set of stoneware dishes, kitchen towels, sheets, cooking utensils, bowls, and numerous other items they would need. After the last guest had left and her parents had gone as well, Alexis and Cliff lingered over the pile of gifts. Now that the cabin had been cleaned up, Alexis was excited about moving out all of the old items that had been furnished with the rented rooms and moving in the new.

"How did they think of everything?" Alexis wondered aloud.

"Your mom had a list," Cliff confided. "She wanted to replace all of the old stuff that's been here for years. The guests were really excited about it, too. I'm amazed that you didn't catch on, just from the sparkle in their eyes!"

"I've been too busy to notice anyone," Alexis admitted. "Why did they include you in the surprise?" She walked over to him for a kiss.

He wrapped his arms around her in a big hug. "One of the guests slipped and mentioned it to me! From then on, it was just easier for me to help plan. I snuck over here a few times on assignments from your mom! Since you were always here working, though, I had to pretend I'd come to see you!"

Alexis laughed, remembering the numerous times he had shown up unexpected in the middle of the day. She felt so safe and secure here in Cliff's arms. In their own home. In love.

Finally, the big day arrived. Summer over, the harbor was once again occupied by just Alexis and her family, with an occasional guest. Alexis and her mother had spent the final week going over last-minute details. When Alexis tried on her dress for the umpteenth time, she was again awed by its beauty. *Seems a shame to only wear this once*, she mused.

On her wedding day, Alexis awoke to the sound of her mother humming in the kitchen and the smell of fresh-brewed coffee. She snuggled under the covers for a moment, suddenly realizing it was the last morning she would ever wake up in this house. Tomorrow morning, and every morning after that, she would wake up with Cliff beside her.

Her stomach let out a low rumble, and she quietly rose and looked out the window at the harbor. Though the sun was not visible from her viewpoint, the sunlight was just beginning to shine on the early morning water, causing it to sparkle. The water made the familiar lapping sound as it splashed up against the boats tied to the dock. Alexis was grateful that she would have this same panorama from her new home, as the little cabin's largest bedroom window faced the same direction.

Glancing around the harbor, Alexis was surprised to see someone already up and on the dock. While she watched, the dark, muscular figure drew back his pole and cast his line far out into the water. Alexis gasped. It was Cliff! She suppressed a giggle. Tradition being that the bride and groom were not supposed to see each other until the wedding, she felt fortunate to get this one tiny peak. She wondered if he were as excited as she. She raised a hand to tap on the window, then reconsidered, content to watch him instead.

"Mrs. Cliff Hunter," she whispered, letting the words roll off her tongue. "Alexis Hunter." Shivering at the thought of it, or maybe at the chilliness of the early September morning, she hugged her arms to herself.

"What did you say?" mumbled a sleepy voice from behind her.

Startled, Alexis whirled around. For the moment she had forgotten that Jenny was still asleep in the double bed. She and her husband Eric had arrived the day before, just in time for dinner and the rehearsal. Wanting to spend her last night of singlehood with her friend, Jenny had suggested that Eric share a room with Cliff and his best man.

"Cliff's out on the dock," she whispered.

Jenny jumped out of bed and ran to the window. "Kinda feel like you're getting a sneak preview?" she asked. "You know you guys aren't supposed to see each other until the wedding!"

"What worries me is, with Cliff out on the docks, what are Larry and Eric doing at this moment?" Alexis asked. "Stuffing rice in Cliff's underwear? Decorating the Blazer?" Cliff's best man Larry was quite a practical joker and kept Alexis and her mother more than a little worried that the wedding would go off with no hitches.

"Don't worry, I'll try to keep Eric in tow," Jenny promised with a grin. "As for Larry, I promise nothing, since I don't really know him! You know guys--they think stuff like that is hilarious."

"Yes, and since you were at *my* house all night, there wasn't anyone to watch them in the wee hours of the morning," Alexis reminded her, then laughed. "Oh well, let them have their fun. Besides, turnabout's fair play, and anything Larry does to Cliff, Cliff will do at least as much back to him when *he* gets married!"

Besides, she thought smugly, *tonight, and every night from now on, Cliff is all mine. That's all that matters.*

"I smell coffee," she told her roommate. "Head straight for the kitchen!"

* * *

Chapter Seven

Arriving at the church over an hour ahead of time, Alexis wanted to make certain all of the many arrangements were as they should be. After she and Jenny spoke with the wedding coordinator at the church, Alexis was satisfied that the reception would be just as planned. The three-tiered cake was beautiful, with a ceramic boy and girl dressed in wedding attire to finish off the top tier. Red and pink roses, with tiny green leaves, adorned the fluffy white frosting. Pink cocktail napkins with silver letters reading "Cliff and Alexis Forever" were perfectly arranged on the table next to the cake. Pink and white mints and bowls of mixed nuts sat nearby, and the rented coffee tureen and silver tea set made an attractive array on the end of the beverage table next to the punch.

"You don't by any chance like pink?" teased Jenny, wearing her pink and green floral bridesmaid dress.

Alexis grinned. "Have the flowers arrived yet?" she asked her mother, who had just entered the large room.

"Yes, and they're lovely," said Kate. "I just came to ask you about the candles. Can you come upstairs for a minute?"

Both girls trailed behind her as they walked up the stairs. As they viewed the large sanctuary, Alexis drew a deep breath. "Doesn't that smell wonderful?" The room was beautiful as well. Each pew was decorated by a single long-stemmed rose and baby's breath on the aisle. Large arrangements decorated the front, and Alexis's bouquet was a simple but pretty arrangement of red roses. The box containing corsages and boutonnieres sat on the back pew, and Alexis carefully selected the one she had ordered for her mother to wear.

"Here Mom," she said, preparing to pin it on the outfit Kate had bought especially for the occasion. The pink and maroon corsage, larger than the others, accented the deep magenta of her dress.

Kate's eyes misted. "It's beautiful, dear," she whispered. "And so are you. I've never been happier for you than this moment."

"Thanks, Mom." Alexis felt her chest growing tight but was determined not to give in to tears and run the carefully applied mascara. "Jenny, here's yours." Jenny's corsage was a dainty array of tiny pink and white roses that matched the bridesmaid dress perfectly. "Now, Jenny, when Dad and Cliff and the other bridesmaids arrive, will you please see that they all get their flowers?"

Jenny nodded.

"And Mom, what was it you wanted to know about the candles?"

"Oh! I got sidetracked." Kate showed Alexis the pink rose candle by the guest book. "Is this where you want it?"

Alexis smiled a deep, slow smile. It was fun to see all of their plans come alive. The pink feather pen on a velvet cushion, the pink rose candle, the white guest book with gold lettering.... All of which, Alexis knew, cost her parents a pretty penny.

"It's fine, Mom," she answered. "Just perfect. And now, I suppose I should be getting dressed myself."

Before Alexis knew it, organ music could be heard through the doorway of the dressing room used only by herself. Jenny came in to help her put the finishing touches on her hair, then gave her a light hug and left. Her father knocked timidly at the door, calling her name. "You ready, Alexis?"

She glanced at herself one more time in the mirror. "Coming, Daddy." The long white satin gown was still as beautiful as the many times she had tried it on before the wedding. "This is for real, Alex," she told her reflection.

"What, honey?"

"Nothing! I'll be out in a minute." She placed the old-fashioned tiara on her head, smiling at her promise to Cliff not to wear a veil, and opened the door to walk into the hall.

Rarely had she seen her father cry, but for a moment his eyes blurred, and he did not speak. Then, choking, he said, "I've never seen you more beautiful. I hope Cliff knows what he's getting."

Alexis's own eyes misted, but again she pushed tears back. "Now, Daddy, don't make me cry at my own wedding! I imagine Mom will do that enough for all of us!"

"Well, now, that's for sure," he admitted gruffly. Extending his arm, he said, "Shall we go?"

They walked together into the foyer of the church, empty except for a mother with a crying baby and a couple of ushers, ready to greet late guests at the door. All eyes fixed on her as she and her father waited at the entrance to the sanctuary. The familiar chords of the wedding march were her cue to begin the walk down the aisle. Before doing so, she glanced up on the platform to catch Cliff's eye.

He had been watching for her, and as his eyes caught hers, he flashed her the familiar smile she loved. The white tuxedo made him look irresistibly handsome. She remembered their earlier discussions about his wearing it: his objections and her finally cajoling him into it. She was glad he had given in, as *she* had on a few other details. In the end, the wedding was a blend of both of their ideas. A day Alexis would remember forever.

Taking a deep breath, she began the long walk down the aisle.

She seemed to be floating on a cloud and was barely aware of the songs being sung and the words being said. A friend of theirs sang "Time in a Bottle," Cliff's choice, a less traditional number which at first her mother had objected to. A woman from church sang "Wither Thou Goest," one of Alexis's favorites. As Alexis listened, and did as the pastor said, she was at last aware of him urging her to repeat after him the words that would bind her to Cliff for the rest of her life.

"To have and to hold," the pastor prompted.

Alexis didn't wait for his next prompt, but finished the sentence in one breath. "...to have and to hold, from this day forward, for better or for worse, for richer, for poorer, in sickness and in health, 'til death do us part."

Cliff smiled as his eyes shined into her own.

"Now Cliff, repeat after me," the pastor urged.

"I, Cliff, take thee Alexis," Cliff said solemnly, then repeated the rest of his lines. When it was all over, and they were pronounced man and wife, Eric let out a loud "whoop!" from the audience. Everyone laughed, but Cliff's eyes were serious as he leaned down for their first married kiss.

Jenny, a new bride herself, made a beautiful matron of honor. As Alexis stood in the receiving line at the reception, Jenny met her every need, bringing her punch and taking care of endless details.

"After you guys leave, Eric and I will take all the gifts to the cabin so you can open them after your honeymoon," Jenny told her.

"Did Mom bring my suitcase?" Alexis asked. "I was in such a hurry to get married I forgot it!"

Jenny nodded.

"You're a lifesaver," Alexis told her friend, impulsively giving her a hug.

When it was time to leave, Alexis changed out of the beautiful wedding dress and placed it carefully on a hanger. She dressed quickly in the tan and white traveling suit she had purchased for the occasion and grabbed her suitcase.

Opening the door to meet the waiting crowd, she gave her mother a hug. "Thanks, Mom--for everything," she whispered. She hugged her father, who uncharacteristically had tears in his eyes, and took Cliff's hand.

"Ready?" he asked.

Alexis nodded. Turning her back on the roomful of guests, she threw her bridal bouquet over her shoulder and ran, laughing, through the door. To their surprise, the Blazer had been gaily decorated with flowers and ribbons, with old shoes tied to the vehicle's fender and a large "JUST MARRIED" painted in lipstick across the back window. Alexis just laughed, and Cliff seemed not to mind. Neither did he seem to mind, hours later, when she was still shaking rice out of her negligee, obviously placed there by her helpful matron of honor!

The honeymoon was everything Alexis had hoped for. To have Cliff all to herself--with no restrictions and no interruptions--was almost more than she had dreamed of. The two of them stayed up as late as they wanted, savoring each other's company. Though they visited the lovely Butchart Gardens in Victoria, British Columbia, the sights and sounds and meals they took in were secondary to the wonder of just being together.

After the two weeks were up, Alexis happily settled down to married life in the harbor. Living in the cabin proved to be a good situation for all of them. The young couple was close to Alexis's parents, yet far enough away to have time alone.

Their life together took on a comfortable routine. Each morning they prayed together before leaving the cabin. Daytime kept them both busy with the numerous duties involved in running the resort. During that fall and the following winter, Cliff spent his hours fixing leaky faucets, repairing the docks, and repainting the units. He was never without something to do. When that first winter hit, water pipes froze and burst, and Cliff and Charlie spent weeks repairing the damage.

Alexis tried her hand at gourmet cooking, once again to impress the man she loved. She soon discovered that Cliff, a simple meat and potatoes man, preferred a steak and baked potato to Veal Oscar and Beef Wellington. Cliff's aunt had given them a bread machine for a wedding present, and Alexis delighted in experimenting with all of the various varieties. Once a week, usually on the weekend, the couple ate up at the big house with Alexis's parents.

The second year of their marriage, Alexis began to grow restless for something more than life in the harbor. As business dropped off and prices all over Canada increased, the family could not afford to hire outside maid service. Alexis and her mother kept the sheets and towels washed and rooms cleaned and swept. Fortunately, most of their guests were fishermen who spent a great deal of time on the water and required few special services. There was little time for fishing with Cliff or doing any of the things Alexis really wanted to do. Work took priority, and although she didn't mind pitching in and doing extra, she tired easily and found it difficult to keep her spirits up. Somehow this wasn't the romantic married life she envisioned.

Frustrated that Cliff was working all the time as well, Alexis tried to set aside a couple times a week to take the boat out by herself and catch fish for supper.

"Want to go?" she asked him time after time, trying to tempt him away from his work.

"Sorry, hon," he would usually reply with a tired smile, "can't get away just now. But you go and have a good time."

Funny how marriage changes things, she thought to herself. *I wonder if he'd even notice if I didn't come home!* As little as she saw of Cliff, she would have been better off not marrying him! Before they were married, the two of them spent hours together. Now there was never any time.

Is this all marriage is? she wondered. Well, it wasn't enough for her. But when she tried sharing her feelings with Cliff, the words came out all wrong, and she felt like a nagging wife. Cliff, weary from a hard day's work, never seemed to understand her unhappiness. Just the night before she had approached him during supper.

"Cliff, I need more of you," she told him honestly.

"What do you mean? I see you at night after work, like most married couples," he replied, helping himself to a second piece of fried chicken.

"We are not 'most married couples'" she retorted angrily. "A maid could do what I do! You don't come home to *me* any longer--you come home to a hot meal and a warm bed! Would you even notice if I weren't here?"

She blinked back tears, then continued. "Sometimes I feel like you love life in the harbor more than you love me."

He had brushed her off, saying, "Alex, don't be ridiculous. Of course, I love the harbor, and your parents--and I love YOU. For Pete's sake, you're my WIFE!"

"If you had to choose, would you choose me or the harbor?" she asked bluntly.

"I don't have to choose," he replied calmly.

Frustrated, she began to cry. "I have to get away from here," she told him. "You had your chance--you went to college. I've never done anything but this. I didn't even get to finish nursing school."

Cliff, uncertain how to respond, replied, "Alexis, I'm too tired to deal with this. Let's just get through the summer, okay?" He pushed his chair away from the table, wiped his mouth with a napkin, and stood. "Good dinner, hon," he said sincerely.

Alexis did not respond. That night, like so many times before, she went to bed early and cried herself to sleep.

* * *

Chapter Eight

Cliff yawned. He shivered in the cool morning air and turned over to snuggle with his wife. They had both been working so hard lately; he understood her demand for more attention but was usually too tired to give it to her. He was surprised to find her side of the bed empty, though. According to the luminous numbers on the clock it was still too early for her to be up. Not hearing her in the bathroom, he lay there a moment thinking.

Alexis had been in the strangest mood lately. Nothing seemed to calm her down. The most inconsequential things set her off, and when Cliff tried to soothe her, she only became more irate.

What disturbed him even more were her accusations. Cliff was content with his life and work in the harbor, and Alexis accused him of loving the lifestyle more than he loved her.

Like last night, for example. "If you had to choose, would you choose me or the harbor?" she had asked.

Cliff shook his head, again puzzled at the question. He did not understand her outbursts. Why didn't women come with a "how-to" manual on how to handle them?

He knew that Kate had tried to understand her daughter's moodswings. "What would you rather be doing, honey?" his mother-in-law had asked Alexis one day in his presence, while Cliff, frustrated, pretended to turn a deaf ear. Alexis simply answered that she didn't know. She just wanted a chance to find out. Her words last night rang in his head, "Would you even notice if I weren't here?"

Suddenly reality dawned on Cliff, and he jumped out of bed. The cabin was quiet except for the monotonous dripping of the kitchen faucet that Alexis had so often nagged him about. "The plumber's faucet is the last to be fixed," she had said. Cliff walked down the hallway, through the kitchen, and into the living room. No sign of Alexis anywhere. He turned to go back to the bedroom when his eye caught a glance of her familiar handwriting on an envelope on the kitchen table.

Tearing open the flap, he withdrew the letter and read:

Dear Cliff,

    I have to get away for a while. I'm sorry to hurt you, but I need some time to myself.

Don't worry about me, and *don't* try
to find me. I'll be back in a couple of
weeks.

Yours,
Alex

Cliff pounded his fist on the table, knocking over
the salt and pepper shakers. She had really done it!
She'd gone and left him. He hadn't taken her seriously
before, but now he wished he had. Maybe he could
have talked her out of going.

Throwing on a pair of jeans, he pulled a T-shirt
over his head and stepped into his tennis shoes.
Running up the hill to the big house, he burst in the
front door without knocking.

"Cliff--what is it?" Kate was sitting at the kitchen
table drinking a cup of coffee. "It's not even six-thirty
yet. Is everything all right?"

Just then the door opened. It was Charlie. "Kate,
the Seaswirl's gone! Someone's taken Alexis's boat!"
Surprised to see his son-in-law, he stared at Cliff.

"Hi, Dad," Cliff said grimly. "We have to talk."

Over coffee and scones, he showed them the letter,
and they spent an hour discussing what to do. Cliff
shook his head. "I didn't believe she would really
leave," he said sadly. "What's the matter with her?"

Then, glancing over at Kate, he said, "You're a woman. Do you understand her?"

"She *did* mention it before," her mother answered in her daughter's defense, "but I didn't realize it was this serious."

"Well, what am I supposed to do?" Cliff yelled. "The letter says not to look for her. Maybe she just went on a vacation." He shook his head. "I wonder if--" He paled.

"Don't even think it," said Kate, placing a steady hand on his arm. "There's no one but you, dear, you know that. Alexis may be high-strung, but she would never be unfaithful."

* * *

Alexis drifted for a while, until it became light enough for her to see without the boat's headlights. She would reach her destination within the next hour or two. Hopefully she would arrive in time for breakfast, as her stomach was already beginning to complain. Had it not been so risky, she would gladly have made a pot of coffee to bring a thermos along. She shivered.

Weeks ago, when she first entertained thoughts of leaving the harbor, the question was always where to go. Then she remembered the many times she had seen the Malibu Princess floating by, its happy occupants waving to her. She spent a memorable week at Malibu Club the summer she was fifteen, just before Cliff left for his first year of college. The week had been a mountaintop experience she had never forgotten.

Malibu Club was a camp for young people, located near the entrance to the Princess Louisa Inlet of British Columbia, a hundred miles north of Vancouver. The remote property was one place Cliff wouldn't think of looking for her--if he looked at all--though he would probably check with everyone they both knew in Vancouver. When the flyer and registration form had come in the mail last month, Alexis seized her golden opportunity. For two weeks in May church groups and individuals went to Malibu for a "Tool and Tackle" week, to prepare the camp for the busy summer. Since Alexis had registered ahead of time, they were expecting her. They would not even know she was a "runaway", Alexis thought wryly. Unless someone she knew from church was there. And, if so, it would be at least a week or two before they could go home and tell anyone they'd seen her. By that time, she would be ready to go home herself.

Or would she?

Alexis didn't understand the war within herself. Her emotions seemed out of balance. Though temperamental as a pre-teen, as an adult Alexis was less emotional than most other women she knew. But lately she was moody and restless, and that in itself frustrated her. Nurses needed to stay calm and level-headed, which was one reason she thought she would have made a good one.

And that was another thing, Alexis mused, studying a boat approaching from behind to determine whether she knew the driver. It didn't help matters any that she had never finished nursing school. Had finances been better, and if she weren't needed so much at home, she would talk to Cliff about returning to her studies. Before marriage she had thought Cliff was all she wanted, but somehow, he just wasn't enough. Had she given in too quickly? Perhaps she should have finished school before marrying at all.

The boat sped by, and the driver waved to her. She waved back, wondering if he, too, were headed to the camp. Because of its remote location, Malibu seemed at the end of the earth. But she knew it was there, waiting for her.

After thirty minutes Alexis passed two boats with fishing lines dangling over the side. One of the men looked familiar, but she sped ahead. She didn't care if Cliff knew where she was--as long as he left her alone.

Now that it was light, Alexis marveled at the rugged beauty surrounding her. Waterfalls cascaded down both sides of the inlet, reminding her of pictures she had seen of the Fjords in Norway. The biggest waterfall she had ever seen was just past Malibu, down at the national park. Hopefully she would have time later in the week for sightseeing.

Rounding a curve, Alexis let out a sigh. There was Malibu, straight ahead! It was exactly as she remembered. Morning fog hovered around the camp like a shroud, giving it an air of mystery. The complex of buildings sat on high rock cliffs connected by boardwalks. From the short film she had seen that summer years ago, she knew that in the 1940s the resort had been frequented by such famous guests as John Wayne and Walt Disney. In the early 1950s it was transformed into a Young Life camp.

Each week Young Life's own travel ship, the Malibu Princess, carried a new group of 200 teenage campers to Malibu, then transported the previous week's campers back to Vancouver. Alexis had not ridden the Malibu Princess the year she had attended camp. Her father and mother had taken her in their own boat, then stayed a while for a tour of the premises. The two of them might consider the camp as a possible hideout, but Alexis doubted it.

She slowed the boat down and drove around back to the long float, carefully avoiding the entrance to the right where she knew rocks hid just under the surface. As she pulled up to the float, she noticed a short, stocky man in white jeans and a blue pullover sweatshirt ready to guide the boat in.

"Welcome to Malibu!" he greeted as she came within hearing distance. He helped her tie the boat, then took the suitcase from her hand and helped her onto the dock.

"Thanks!" Alexis stopped to view her surroundings. Improvements had obviously been made since she was here the last time, but otherwise the place was as she remembered. A brightly painted totem pole with strange colorful designs and faces stood in the center of the deck. Long walkways extended upward on both sides of the main dock, and a Canadian flag flapped in the early morning breeze.

"I'm Victor," the man offered, extending a hand.

"Hi, I'm Alex--I mean, Alexis. I'm here for the work weeks."

"Well, Alex, I mean Alexis, you're just in time for breakfast," he teased. "Let's take your bag and go on up to the dining room."

"Oh, good, I'm dying for some coffee!" she moaned. "Is my boat okay here?"

"Sure. You should come back later today and put the hood on, in case it rains. But for now, it's fine." The man, much older than herself, had a mop of unruly gray hair, and she detected a strong British accent. That was one thing she liked about living in Canada. Some people spoke with no accent at all; others sounded like they were straight out of Great Britain.

They walked together up the ramp to the long upward deck and entered the dining room just as someone said "Amen" after the morning prayer.

Alexis sucked in her breath in awe as her gaze took in the tall, paneled windows on three sides of the dining hall and the majestic fireplace in the middle of the room. She had forgotten it was so beautiful. Glancing around, she noticed that most people were already seated at the various tables and had dished up their food. Unsure of herself, she glanced over at Victor.

"Have a seat," Victor offered with a smile. "You can get your room assignment after breakfast. I have work to finish, so I'll see you later. Your suitcase is just outside the door."

Alexis thanked him and walked over to a table near the window with several other women. She immediately poured herself a cup of coffee, then filled her plate with fresh fruit. Hot biscuits steamed under a cloth in a straw basket, and the thick, hot Red River cereal, a camp favorite, filled a bowl in the middle of the table. Though many liked it, the cereal reminded her of bird seed, and she preferred instead cold cereal or eggs. This morning the main entree was broccoli quiche, which Alexis loved. She occasionally took the time to prepare it for herself and Cliff, but he would rather have pancakes and bacon every day of his life.

Cliff. Alexis shook her head. She had to stop thinking about him. After all, she came here to get away, didn't she?

The other women introduced themselves. Alexis was surprised to learn that most of the people in the room lived at the camp, at least from May through September. Church groups would not be arriving until midday.

"What are you going to do this week?" one of the women asked. She had said her name was Cathy, and she worked in the camp's office.

"I--I don't really know," Alexis mumbled. "I don't do carpentry or mechanics, but I could clean, or help with laundry."

"We always need that." Cathy chuckled. "Or you could assist Nadine if you want. This morning she's going to visit every room and make sure the curtains are in good shape and that each bed has a coverlet."

"Oh, that sounds like fun! I could see the entire camp that way, couldn't I!" Alexis's blue eyes sparkled at the thought.

"It *is* fun. There are rooms here that most people never see because they're always full of guests," Cathy told her. "Right now, the place is virtually empty. Do you want me to introduce you to Nadine?"

"Yes, please." The awkwardness of meeting new people was gone, and Alexis began to consider the next two weeks as something other than an escape. After all, she *was* here to work.

"What else would you be interested in doing?" Cathy probed as they walked down the boardwalk after the delicious meal. Carrying Alexis's suitcase, Cathy showed Alexis to her room, a simple cabin with two bunks that she should share with another female worker.

"Well, I'm not good at gardening," Alexis admitted, then hesitated. "To be truthful, I had hoped for a job with the boats. I've been fishing and boating since I was five. Does the camp ever need a driver?"

"Hmmm, not really," Cathy replied. "Later on in the week we'll take a trip down the inlet to the national park and the waterfall. But Dennis Feldman drives the boat for that. He's the camp manager. You might ask him about helping. While the groups are here, they are encouraged to take a boat out and go fishing or grab a canoe."

Alexis smiled. So, the weeks wouldn't be *all* work! She was beginning to feel more relaxed already.

They found Nadine at the entrance to the laundry room. Alexis burst out laughing as she read the sign just above her head. "Heeranweewashum?" she questioned. "An Indian term?"

"Malibu English for 'here we wash the clothes'!" Nadine teased.

"Nadine, you missed breakfast!" Cathy scolded.

"Oh, I had a bowl of Red River in my quarters," Nadine admitted. "I got up late." She glanced over at Alexis and extended a hand. "Hi."

"Hi. I'm Alexis. Cathy said you might need some help."

Cathy left for the office. Nadine, grateful for the unexpected assistance, kept up a running commentary as they spent the morning visiting the various rooms. Alexis was impressed at the simplicity of many of the cabins and the sheer luxury of others. One apartment in particular had matching redwood furniture, its own bathroom, and two bedrooms joined by a sitting room.

"Wow," she commented as she explored the quarters, running a hand over the expensive-looking wood.

"Yeah, *wow*. They call this one the 'Honeymoon Cottage'. William Holden and his wife spent their honeymoon here," Nadine informed her. "Though no one seems to be sure *which* room it really was, they know it was one of them!" she admitted. "Malibu had many famous guests in the old days."

"It's really beautiful. Especially being up here on the third deck. Very private." She thought for a moment how nice it would be if she and Cliff could get away to a place like this.

Close to noon they headed back to the laundry nook with their report. In the afternoon they would visit the other cabins, Nadine told her, but it was almost lunchtime. When the two of them entered the dining hall, Alexis was amazed at all of the newcomers. Most of the tables were filled, and they scanned the room for a place they could sit together.

After a hearty lunch of fresh homemade tomato soup, toasted cheese sandwiches, and salad, Mr. Feldman appeared up in front to make several announcements. He encouraged everyone in the group to get acquainted and announced that the trip to the waterfall would be on Thursday.

Next Frank, the camp's experienced cook, stood up to say that he still needed one more helper for supper and two table setters. One more person was needed to work in the dish pit after lunch as well.

Alexis's hand shot up when Frank asked for a volunteer to help with supper. He gave her an appreciative smile and said, "Thanks--report for work at four o'clock."

At least that was one thing she knew how to do, Alexis told herself. She certainly was used to helping her mother in the kitchen and felt like she was well on her way to becoming a good cook in her own right.

After clearing her lunch dishes and separating them into the large plastic tubs for washing, she noticed a group of women gathering at a table near the fireplace. They appeared to be tying knots in wire cords, and she watched for a few minutes in fascination. Finally, she walked over to the table and asked, "What are you doing?"

"Tying clasps," one replied. "For bead necklaces for crafts. Want to help?"

"Mmmm. Maybe tomorrow. Today's already full. That *is* one thing I'd like to do, though. Is it hard?"

The woman laughed. "If I can do it, anyone can! The only thing tough about it is the callouses left on your hand when you're done!"

Smiling, Alexis left to rejoin Nadine, who was waiting for her by the door.

"Well, where to next?" she asked. "I'm yours 'til four o'clock!"

The afternoon flew by. They walked together to each room, then separated to check curtains and coverlets. Nadine scribbled hasty notations on a clipboard for reporting back to the group of women sewing for the week. Four o'clock soon came, and Alexis reported to Frank for kitchen duty. He quickly put her to work peeling carrots and chopping lettuce for a huge green salad as well as mixing batter for cornbread to accompany that evening's beans and frankfurters.

Reasoning that she was there to help, she assisted in serving supper as well, then volunteered for dish pit. Alexis was pleased to note that Victor, her first acquaintance at Malibu, was captain of the dish pit and orchestrated his assistants with obvious experience. In spite of the many plates, cups, salad bowls, pieces of flatware, as well as the heavy pots and pans, Victor kept the procession moving at a rapid pace. To Alexis's amazement, the group of eight finished in an hour.

"You've done this before!" she told Victor, stating the obvious.

"Over thirty years," Victor replied. "Three meals a day. Just for the work weeks. Got to keep it moving or you'll be here all night!" He gave her a warm smile. "Barking orders seems to be what I'm best at!"

Alexis gave him a warm smile. "You weren't in the military, by any chance, were you?" she quipped, then laughed. Hanging the plastic apron over a hook on the back of the door, she left for her cabin.

After climbing three sets of stairs, she stood overlooking the inlet. The view from the upper deck was breathtaking. Though not yet dark, a sliver of a moon peaked over a tall mountain to the west. It was difficult for Alexis to believe it was the same moon that shone over Pender Harbor, which at that moment seemed light years away.

In her room she was pleased to note that her roommate had arrived. A young woman in her early twenties was busy rolling out a sleeping bag.

"Oh, hello!" she said cheerfully to the newcomer, stopping beside the bunk.

The woman turned around and offered Alexis a shy smile. "Hi, I'm Kelsey. From Vancouver. I'm helping with crafts all summer."

Alexis brightened. "Oh! That's what I'm doing tomorrow--tying necklaces. Are you in charge of that?"

Kelsey slowly answered, "Well, not in charge of it exactly, but I brought all the craft stuff over on the boat with me. Tomorrow I'm going to organize it all and stock the cubicles in Totem Trader."

"That sounds like fun! Maybe I could work with you instead. Do you need help?"

Kelsey certainly did need help, Alexis mused the next morning as she assisted in unpacking carton after carton. Craft supplies for twelve weeks of campers took up quite a large amount of space in the Totem Trader, the camp's own little store. A certain amount of craft supplies was included with the campers' initial fee for the week, then they purchased more as needed.

Mid-afternoon she took some time off to explore the grounds, strolling over by the golf course and past the oyster beds, then down the ramp to visit the boiler room and machinery shop. She was duly impressed, for the operation was certainly self-sustaining. The entire complex was powered by three diesel generators. During the peak evening time a huge generator serviced the area, while in the mornings a smaller one took over. She knew Cliff would have enjoyed touring the layout. Maybe, if he was ever here with her, she could show him around. Maybe....

Already she was planning ahead. Would Cliff be interested in coming to Tool and Tackle the following year? she wondered. His skills would be invaluable here, and she knew he would enjoy meeting the people and putting his crafts to use.

Alexis shook the thoughts away. *First, let's just get through THIS year, Alex!* she told herself. *This WEEK! Remember, you came here to get AWAY from Cliff!*

Necklace-tying occupied the following day, and by suppertime she understood just what the woman meant about callouses. The wire cord cut against the side of her hand where she pulled the knot tight. Her hands red and raw, she decided against volunteering for dish pit but offered to set the table for breakfast the next morning.

Setting plates on the red and white tablecloth, she overheard a conversation going on at the next table. Over the clinking of flatware, it seemed the two were discussing going somewhere early the next morning. Thinking it was fishing, she began to listen in.

"And don't forget to wear boots," the man informed the woman. "Deck shoes don't have enough traction."

"Who all is going?" the woman asked.

"Oh, the usual group. The couple from Massachusetts--they moved a couple of years ago, you know, but come back every year just for Malibu-- several women you probably don't know, Betty, James and Frieda, and a few others."

Curious, Alexis tried to get a little closer without being rude.

"Have I talked you into it yet?" the man asked.

"I don't know, Stan," replied the woman. "I haven't even had my coffee at that hour!"

"Excuse me," Alexis began, taking advantage of the break, "but is there a group going fishing in the morning?"

Stan's face turned into a smile. He was about twice her age, a little man with a mustache that twitched when he smiled. "No, my dear, the daily hike to Inspiration Point."

"Inspiration Point? Where's that?"

"Follow me." He laid down the fork he was holding and beckoned her to the door.

"Oh no, Stan has a new audience," remarked the woman he'd been talking to, laughing.

They walked outside and down the long deck, stopping just before the stairs. "Look," he said pointing, "up there!"

Alexis followed his line of vision. There, up on the hillside, was a lookout point cordoned off by rope attached to metal stakes.

"Way up there?" She gasped. "How long does it take to hike?"

"Half an hour or so," Stan told her. "You interested?"

"Well...." She hesitated. "I thought you were going fishing. I didn't mean to butt in."

"Anyone's welcome. We try to discourage children because of the danger, but anyone else is welcome."

"Danger?"

"Since it only takes half an hour to climb, it's very steep," Stan informed her. "There's a large fallen tree to walk on, as well as rocks to climb."

"You mean, like scaling the side of a mountain?" Alexis asked.

Stan's mustache twitched as he tried not to laugh. "No, not at all. The only real danger is falling, but not falling off the edge. At one point there's a rope to hold on to, to pull yourself up the mountain. It's steep, but not treacherous." His eyes twinkled. "Are you game?"

"Let me think about it," she told him. "I could use some exercise. Where would I meet everyone?"

After finishing up her kitchen duties, Alexis walked up to her room thinking it over. More than anything she was curious. The idea was tantalizing. She thought of the early morning air slapping her face, and she could only imagine the view from the top.

Taking in the breathtaking site the next morning, Alexis decided that the grueling climb had definitely been worth it. As the group rested at the top, Alexis pulled out her cell phone and snapped several shots of the complex lying far below. She noted a new text from Cliff she decided to read later, when she was alone.

The hike was everything Stan had said it would be. The fallen tree, the rocks, the rope guide. Alexis had taken the climb slow and easy, not wanting to pull a muscle or wear herself out for the rest of the week. The woman from Massachusetts was kind enough to wait for her and guide her along.

"Impressive, isn't it," the woman, named Florence, said to her. "Brisk and energizing, too. Revs me up for all day! Think you'll come again tomorrow?"

Alexis laughed. "Well, if I don't, I promise I'll walk onto the upper deck at six-thirty so Stan will have someone to wave to," she answered, laughing as Stan was bellowing "hallooed" to unknown persons below.

The next morning, she awoke intending to hike again, but her tired muscles told her otherwise. Instead, she showered, walked to the dining hall for a cup of coffee, then sat in a deck chair waiting for the group to appear at the top. At six-thirty-five, she glanced up and noticed them at the lookout point.

Excited, she almost spilled her coffee standing up. "Hello," she shouted, frantically waving her hands. "Hello! Stan!" She yelled until she caught their attention, and she could hear Stan's loud bellow back to her.

When Thursday arrived, Alexis was more than ready for a boat ride down the inlet. She longed to take the Seaswirl out for a spin just to feel the spray of water on her face. Stepping into the large float boat for the waterfall trip, she realized how different this boat was from any she had seen before. The thing resembled a barge and held up to forty people, standing up, for there were no seats except the driver's. Though Cathy and Nadine had taken the trip numerous times, Alexis was pleased that they were both going again. The women Alexis met from necklace tying went along as well.

The first timers 'ooohed' in wonder at the many sights along the way. An eagle protecting her nest high up on the cliffs glared down at the onlookers as they floated by. Dozens of small waterfalls trickled down the sides of the rock walls.

When they had arrived at a certain point, Mr. Feldman explained that the spot was perfect for echoing. He then yelled out, "Helloooooo!". The group laughed as the voice came back at them, just as clearly, "Helloooooo!" Several of the passengers shouted various phrases, testing the resonating sound bouncing off the rocks.

As the boat rounded a corner, the group "aaahed", and Alexis realized they had arrived at the national park. "Ooooh," she said appreciatively. The waterfall was as beautiful as she remembered. Clear glistening water cascaded down the bank; ferns and other greenery nearby seemed to frame its glory. Alexis stepped off the boat to join the others on the path to view the waterfall more closely. Heeding the warning signs to stay behind the railing, she recalled how, many years ago, a teenage boy helping at the camp had dared fate and stepped beyond the boundaries. His life was lost in the fast-flowing water.

"Hey, Alexis!" She heard someone call, and glanced up just in time to see Cathy snapping her picture.

Alexis laughed. "Let me take yours," she offered, and captured Nadine and Cathy just as a spray of water blew their hair to one side.

Falling into step with Mr. Feldman on the way back down the trail, she seized the opportunity to ask him about helping with the boats.

"What did you have in mind?" he asked, puzzled.

"Well, I'd be happy to take a group for a trip down to the waterfall in my own boat," she offered. "I've got a 17-foot Seaswirl. Maybe people that had to work and didn't have a chance to come today. Or gas all the boats up. Or," she offered tentatively, "I could give them all a good washing."

Mr. Feldman stroked his chin, the hint of a grin playing on his lips. "Now, that's an offer I haven't had before! Are you serious?"

"I wouldn't offer if I wasn't," Alexis assured him. "I want to help, that's why I came. But I'd much rather be doing outside stuff. Can you use me?"

"Actually...since you offered, I *can* use you. Also--" he turned to look at her. "Are you here both weeks?"

She nodded.

"Then my wife, Jan, could probably use your help, too. Late in the week she'll be going back to Earl's Cove, where we keep the speedboats all year. Maybe you could go with her to drive one back!"

Alexis was elated. "I'd be happy to!"

For the short remainder of the two weeks, Mr. Feldman put her in charge of the small fleet of crafts maintained by the camp. Each boat needed fuel, an oil change, and a good washing. It was a job Mr. Feldman usually did himself but was all too happy, though reluctant, to give up.

"I'm not used to a woman doing this sort of thing," he had admitted.

Alexis only laughed.

A week later, his wife Jan asked Alexis to ride with her and drive a speedboat back, along with two others. The small group made an occasion of it, stopping for lunch in the small cafe overlooking the water at the little cove.

"Food's better at camp," Jan said matter-of-factly when the waitress was out of earshot.

The others laughed. "It really is," Alexis admitted. "You'd better hold on to Frank while you can!"

Jan nodded. "Don't we know it!"

Speeding along the water in the fast boat was the most exciting thing Alexis had done during her entire stay. Fortunately, the weather chose to cooperate, and the water was smooth and clear. Forgetting about the hot sun, Alexis ended up with a sunburned face and arms.

That evening after dinner, Alexis relaxed with a group of others outside the dining hall on the deck area by the swimming pool. Noticing Mr. Feldman standing nearby, she started to ask him a question about the speedboats. Before she could open her mouth to speak, however, a voice from nearby called out, "Give you ten bucks to jump in!"

Mr. Feldman turned around, startled. His challenger was none other than Cathy.

Several people started laughing. The pool, a cement hole blasted out of solid rock, had only the day before been drained and cleaned, then refilled. Since it was not heated except by the sun, this late in the evening Alexis had a feeling it would be very cold.

Mr. Feldman glanced down at his clothing, khaki walking shorts and a tan plaid shirt, with socks and tennis shoes. He appeared to be thinking it over.

"Make it fifty and I'll do it," he answered. "But make your cheque payable to Young Life!"

"You've got a deal!" Cathy called out.

By now the crowd was laughing and yelling. Mr. Feldman took off his watch and glasses and handed them to Alexis, then without a word dove into the pool. After the loud splash, the crowd cheered. Mr. Feldman's head bobbed above the surface of the water, then he climbed out, dripping water from his clothing at every step.

Alexis was thoroughly enjoying herself. Work or not, Malibu was just the respite she needed. But the two weeks were quickly drawing to a close. Would she be ready to go home when they ended?

* * *

On Thursday of the last week, Alexis began to grow nervous. She wasn't ready to go home yet. She knew in her heart it was wrong to run from her responsibilities at Pender Harbor, but--she wanted to stay longer. A plan began to take shape in her mind.

She approached Dennis Feldman directly after breakfast on the last morning of her two-week stay. She had given it a lot of thought--she wanted to work through the summer. Should she call home *first*, she wondered, or find out if there even was an opening before she dropped the bomb on Cliff?

Mr. Feldman, a man at least ten years her senior, was thoughtful as she rambled on nervously in his office. "I'm sorry," she told him, "Obviously I'm not used to applying for jobs! But I'd really like to work until the beginning of September. I'll do whatever needs to be done."

The camp manager stroked his chin. "Anything?"

"Try me."

"Well, it's funny you should come by. I just found out my laundry person is leaving in a week. How are you at washing sheets?"

Alexis gulped. She had said "anything"--but laundry? The one chore she disliked the most. Hesitating only a second, she replied, "I'll take it." The job was her only chance, and if she didn't snatch it, it would be gone.

"There's one more thing," Mr. Feldman began slowly, stroking his chin between his fingers.

"Yes?"

He patiently explained to her that, whether the job was laundry, cooking, or counseling, each staff person had to be committed to Christ.

"If you mean, am I a Christian, yes," Alexis answered honestly. "I received Jesus into my heart as a little girl. Though I admit I've made mistakes along the way...I always know that God is there for me, and I've tried to make choices that honor Him." She paused, and considered telling him that she wanted her life always to honor and glorify God, but that she wasn't even sure what her life was right now. Or what she should do with it.

She opened her mouth to say more, then, thinking better of it, pressed her lips together and glanced up at him expectantly.

"Okay." He seemed satisfied with her answer and extended his hand. "Welcome to Malibu."

For the next few minutes, they discussed her pay and responsibilities, and what the schedule would be after campers arrived. "Mandy will need to train you," he told her, "But since you hadn't planned on staying so long, you're more than welcome to take a day or two for a trip home for more clothes, if you wish."

"Thanks, but that won't be necessary," Alexis told him. The meeting at an end, she rose to leave.

Mr. Feldman frowned. "Alexis, I--"

"Yes?"

"I sense a restlessness in you. Whatever you came to Malibu hoping to find--I hope you find it." Then he smiled, and looked deep into Alexis's eyes as though he could see into her soul. It was the way her pastor at home always made her feel.

"Thank you," she answered sincerely, amazed at his spiritual insight. "I hope so, too."

Relieved the encounter was over, Alexis headed to her room to gather her thoughts, dreading the phone call to Cliff. She waited until late in the evening when she knew he would be in the house alone and not eating supper with her parents.

"Alex, where ARE you? I'm going crazy worrying about you," Cliff's voice boomed through the phone.

"Cliff, I told you not to worry. I'm fine." She paused, then quietly replied. "I'm at Malibu."

"Malibu. California?"

"No, Camp Malibu. You remember, I told you about that summer when I was fifteen, the camp I went to?"

Cliff was silent for a moment, then retorted, "You're at Malibu? I've been worried out of my mind, and you're at a lush resort two hours away?"

Alexis fought tears. "Cliff, I called to tell you--I'm not ready to come home yet. I took a job here, through the first week of September. Please don't be mad. I don't want to fight." She wanted to say more, but there would be time for that later.

"When you do come home, I might not still be waiting. What do you think of that?"

"Cliff, please--try to understand."

"What is there to understand? You left me, Alex. You left your mom and dad, too. This place is going to be real busy in a week or two. You ditched all your responsibilities. Do you know what this is doing to your mother?" With that, the call disconnected.

After Cliff had hung up, Alexis burst into tears. She had *so* hoped he would understand. Knowing she was letting her parents down as well, she called them and tried to explain.

Kate was sympathetic. "Cliff is here now, honey," she told Alexis, keeping her voice low. "Daddy and I will get by okay. We just want you to be happy. But honey, you have to come home and face the music sometime. Whatever problems you and Cliff are facing must be worked out. Though marriage has its difficult times, try to think back to how much you wanted Cliff in the first place. How you prayed for him not to forget you."

Alexis could hardly speak through her tears. "I know, Mom. I don't really understand what's going on. Don't worry, Cliff and I will work it out. It will do him good to be without me for a while." She paused. "Tell Daddy I love him, okay?"

"Okay, dear."

Alexis ended the call, suddenly very tired.

Her roommate was a little surprised at Alexis's decision to stay. "Doesn't your husband mind you being away so long?" she asked one evening as they lay on their bunk beds in the darkness. Kelsey was already missing her boyfriend, who had chosen to work at a different camp up in Alaska.

"Well...I think by now he'd like to have me home," Alexis answered truthfully, "but I made a commitment and I'm going to stick to it."

Kelsey made no comment, for which Alexis was grateful.

* * *

Chapter Nine

By the end of the second week of camp, Alexis was already exhausted. The camp kept up a hectic pace, and because the Princess brought a new load of campers with every arrival, there was no time to rest between camps. Sleeping bags would take up too much space, so campers were asked not to bring them. Instead, each bed was freshly made up each week. The piles of laundry did not go away. Sheets were weekly, but towels appeared in the bin daily.

One day Nadine, standing nearby watching the teenagers unload, let out a loud sigh. Alexis laughed.

"I was just thinking about next year," Nadine told her. "If she doesn't slow down, the Princess will have to be replaced--she's wearing out. But by then Young Life's new headquarters in Egmont will be finished."

"Oh, I didn't realize that," Alexis said thoughtfully. "Actually, I don't know much about Young Life at all except for Malibu. Did they build something?"

"No, they took over the old fish processing plant. I think it'll work out super for everyone! It's SOOOO much closer than Vancouver. Since the kids don't come from so far, they only have to be on the boat about three hours. And the best part is-- every time the teenagers leave, we'll have a few hours of peace and quiet before the next group!" She chuckled. "I like teenagers as much as the next person, but I could use a little solitude now and then!"

Alexis smiled. To her, Malibu was a nice blend of commotion and stillness. Since the campers had to get up early, and curfew was enforced, by ten-thirty the grounds were usually so quiet one could hear the lapping of the water against the shore. Alexis was fond of sitting on the bench on the deck outside her cabin, just breathing the night air and taking in the view.

Alexis was very much enjoying her busy life at Malibu. When the second week of June arrived, though, she felt a touch of homesickness. This was the first time she had spent a birthday away from her family. She vowed not to mention the occasion to anyone.

At lunchtime when a hundred voices suddenly broke into a chorus of "Happy Birthday," her mouth dropped open in surprise.

"But--but--how did anyone find out?" she sputtered.

Cathy, sitting nearby, called out, "Don't you remember--I saw your driver's license the day you checked in for Tool and Tackle!"

Alexis had forgotten and had no idea why Cathy needed to see her driver's license in the first place. No matter. She was glad that Cathy *had* seen it, and at least someone cared enough to celebrate her birthday. When Frank and another man carried a large cake into the dining room, with more candles than she could count, she burst out laughing. Taking a deep breath, she exhaled, and blew hard. All but several candles flickered, then went out, but they soon burst into flame again. Puzzled, Alexis blew again. When the candles repeated their performance, she started giggling. Trick candles!

A large floral card from her mother arrived in the mail that afternoon, with a short letter enclosed. Alexis, hungry for news from home, began to read her mother's handwriting:

Alexis dear,

> *I'm sorry you can't be home for your birthday this year. Your father and I miss you very much but trust that you are well and happy. We are praying that you'll get things sorted out and will be ready to come home soon.*

> *The harbor is busy as usual, but we are managing fine. Some of the customers have asked about you--they*

still remember that slimy yellow T-shirt you used to wear!

Enclosed is a small check. I remembered the Totem Trader and those hand-woven sweaters you liked so much. I hope you can find something to use the money on. (Or maybe a new romance novel?! Find a good one to bring home!)

Take care, honey. We love you.

Mom and Dad

P.S. Do you realize this is your first birthday away from home?

Alexis blinked back tears and hugged the letter to her heart. Her mother, though most likely hurt at her daughter's departure, still had only loving words to say. Kate had not mentioned Cliff--Alexis was saddened to think that he might still be angry. She was tempted to call him again, but what else was there to say? Now that she had taken on the job, she would see her responsibility through to the end of the summer. Alexis hoped that her parents, as well as Cliff, would understand.

Even if she wasn't certain that *she* did.

* * *

Alexis was feeling quite pleased with herself at the way her freshly baked cinnamon coffeecake had turned out. She let out a long sigh of satisfaction and pondered "testing" it. Sampling the freshly baked goods was one of the few rewards for working in the kitchen, she told herself. Then, reconsidering, she remembered how tightly her jeans had been fitting lately. No coffeecake for her this morning. She covered the large trays with cloths and headed for the laundry room.

Since Frank had been fighting a cold that week, he had immediately taken Alexis up on her offer to help with the three meals and two snacks provided each day. Alexis was glad that her mother had had the patience to teach her a few things--despite Alexis's protests at a younger age. She only hoped her energy would last--the laundry was waiting!

In the laundry room, she pushed another big load of towels into the washing machine from the endless pile on the floor and stopped to catch her breath. Irony, she thought wryly--pure irony. At the harbor she had hated the indoor work. If only her mother could see her now! Running away for a better life...and she was doing laundry! She was grateful she hadn't had to explain *that* on the phone to Cliff! He would have laughed in her face!

"Hi."

Startled, Alexis glanced up to find Crissy standing in the doorway. She was one of the few teenagers Alexis had befriended. A new group of teenagers arrived each week, and it was becoming more and more difficult to remember anyone's name.

"Crissy--hi! Don't you have activities right now?"

The red-haired girl kicked the toe of her tennis shoe against the door jam. "I do, but--I'm not feeling very well."

"Then why don't you go see the nurse?" Alexis asked.

Crissy shrugged. "I, uh--actually I came to talk to you."

Alexis smiled. "I'm honored! Mind if we work while we talk? I'm doing double duty this week."

Crissy listened to Alexis's brief instructions, and they both worked quietly for a few minutes. Crissy began folding towels while Alexis added soap to the washing machine.

"How do you like camp so far?" Alexis asked, shoving a load of sheets into the big gas dryer.

"It's okay." Crissy replied.

"How about the food?"

"The food's good. Especially that broccoli quiche we had yesterday. Kind of made my stomach queasy, though."

Alexis squinted. Funny. It had made *her* stomach queasy, too. She had prepared the quiche--she certainly hoped she didn't unwittingly poison any of the campers!

She merely answered, "I'm glad you liked it. It's one of my favorite recipes. You see, I'm helping the cook out this week every chance I get. He's fighting a bad cold and has been trying to get some extra rest."

Crissy was silent again. For someone who wanted to talk, Alexis mused, Crissy certainly wasn't holding up her end of the conversation. Alexis walked over to her and touched her arm. "Honey--did you want to talk to me about something?"

The girl broke into sobs and Alexis held her shaking body close. "It's okay, sweetie. It's okay."

"Alexis, I think I'm pregnant," Crissy blurted.

Alexis's heart stopped as the words sunk in. Crissy couldn't be more than 15 or 16, and obviously frightened. And, Alexis would have guessed, too shy to carry on a meaningful relationship with a boy.

They sat down on a nearby pile of dirty laundry and Alexis handed her a box of tissues. "Do you want to tell me about it?" she asked gently. The girl's blunt-cut red hair glistened in the bright laundry room lights. *She looks so vulnerable*, Alexis thought. *Much too young to be a wife. And certainly too young to be a mother.*

Crissy's face turned white with fear, and her hands trembled. "You probably won't believe me if I tell you," she declared. "No one else does."

"You've told other people?"

"Just my mom."

"And what did she say?"

Crissy was silent.

"Crissy--I can only help you if you'll let me."

"I was raped." Crissy blurted. "By my stepdad."

Alexis felt like she'd been punched in the stomach. It was one thing to conceive a child in love, in marriage, and quite another to have one out of wedlock. But to have been raped, and by her own stepfather! Alexis shivered at the horror of it.

"You--you told your mother?" she probed.

"Yes. At least, I tried to tell her he messed with me, but she brushed me off. Told me I would have to get used to him, because he was there to stay."

"He 'messed' with you?"

Crissy nodded, her body shaking with violent sobs. "He-- they've only been married for a year. It happened...while she was at work. She works nights. He...came into my room...." She began to sob again. "I've felt creepy for as long as he's been around...but he's never actually DONE it to me before. Once he started to touch me on the front of my sweater--ya know?" She glanced up at Alexis for understanding. "Alexis, I'm tellin' the truth. I'd swear on a Bible. What should I do?"

Lunch was minus two eaters that day, and Alexis was grateful that she need not be present to serve lunch as well as help prepare it. As she and Crissy huddled together in the steamy room, Crissy poured out her heart. After much discussion and prayer, Alexis agreed to try to talk to Crissy's mother.

"Now, let me understand this--does she know you're pregnant?" Alexis asked.

"No, not exactly. When she didn't believe me about the other stuff, I didn't tell her the rest. And I'm not, for sure--I mean, I haven't had the test, but a girl at school was pregnant, and she had all the same symptoms." Crissy paused. "She had hers taken care of."

"She *what*?"

"She had an abortion. Do you think I should do that?"

Alexis, seizing the moment, chose her words carefully. "Crissy, as horrible as your situation is, I don't believe it would be morally right for you to terminate the pregnancy. Do you realize that abortion is actually killing another living human being?"

Crissy looked puzzled. "But at school they told us it's just a blob of tissue. That it's not a baby until it's three months at least. Mine's probably only two at the most."

Alexis scraped her memory for the verse in Psalms. "Crissy, God's Word tells us it's a human being from the very moment it was conceived. Now listen to me. Let's see what we can do about your mom, first of all. As for the baby--there are people all over the world who would love to have a baby to call their own and for one reason or another aren't able to conceive. Would you be willing to carry the child full term, then give it up?" She breathed a silent prayer while waiting for Crissy's response.

Crissy shrugged. "I guess so. I can't keep it, that's for sure."

It wasn't until much later, after she and Crissy had spoken to Crissy's cabin counselor and they had all called Crissy's mother, and Alexis was lying on her cot staring up into the darkness, that Crissy's words echoed in her mind. *"...kind of made my stomach queasy."* Alexis considered the broccoli quiche, and the way her jeans had been fitting so snugly lately and sat up straight in the bed. "Oh my gosh--I'm PREGNANT!"

Her roommate, awakened by the sudden outburst, spoke into the darkness. "Alexis--are you all right?"

Alexis broke into hysterical laughter. "I--I think I'm pregnant!"

Her roommate was quiet, then ventured, "Is that good?"

"Well, yes, but boy, is my husband going to be surprised!"

After the initial shock wore off, Alexis tried to come to terms with her pregnancy. What would Cliff think? she wondered. Considering the matter, she decided that he would be happy. Neither was in a hurry to start a family, but maybe a child was what their marriage needed. Living in the harbor had not been enough for Alexis. Maybe a baby would bring new meaning into her life.

Forgetting for the moment her own condition, Alexis concerned herself with what to do about Crissy. Her immediate plan was for Crissy to stay at Malibu as long as possible. After a long talk with Mr. Feldman and other decision-making staff members regarding

Crissy staying at the camp, Mr. Feldman told Alexis they would let her know the following day. The next morning, he called her aside to announce that Crissy would be allowed to stay for the time being, as long as Alexis would assume responsibility for her. When that week's campers left Crissy could move in with Kelsey and Alexis for the rest of the summer.

Crissy was elated. She confided that she had been afraid to return home, and staying at camp--with Alexis--was the answer to her prayers. A doctor confirmed that she was pregnant, and, based on the circumstances Crissy had described, due date was December. Ironically, Crissy herself had been a Christmas baby, which was why her parents named her as they had. Her father abandoned them when Crissy was just a baby, leaving a young mother to support herself and a young child.

Alexis protectively took Crissy under her wing, though she soon discovered that Crissy had an indomitable spirit most girls her age did not possess. Crissy had been taking care of herself for years, she told Alexis, since the early departure of her father had required her mom being away from home most of Crissy's waking hours.

Crissy became an eager helper in the kitchen, a cook's favorite because she needed only minimal instructions to do the job right the first time. Frank told Alexis it was a trait he wished all of the summer workers had.

Alexis marveled at how Crissy could just go on with her life, not looking back. She was certain that, under the same circumstances, she would be nowhere as calm as the young teen. But Crissy confided one evening that at least here at the camp she knew people cared about her--and she felt safe. From almost the first day her stepfather had moved in, she sensed something not quite right, and lived in fear that something would happen.

"He gave me the creeps from the start," Crissy admitted. "When Mom's around, he acts all nice and proper, but other times he'd 'accidentally' brush up against me or try the doorknob when I was in the bathroom." She shivered. "I tried to put a lock on my bedroom door but wasn't very successful. Mom found out and told me she could have HIM put one on for me. Well, of course he never got around to it!"

Alexis's heart went out to the girl. In contrast, she thought about her own home life, which, typically for a child, she had taken for granted. Her parents were not considered the norm anymore, as they had been married for over forty years and were still very much in love--in fact, more so than ever before. Kate had told Alexis once that a different kind of love replaces the starry-eyed excitement young couples experience when they first marry. Though not as exciting as the initial attraction, the deeper, committed-friendship type of love her parents shared was for a lifetime. Their love was one of mutual admiration and meeting each other's needs. Alexis, growing up, had felt that love very strongly, and the occasional moments when she had entered a room unannounced and caught her parents in an embrace had not been forgotten. It made her feel all the more loved and secure.

These and other thoughts floated through Alexis's mind as she lazily relaxed in a lounge chair near the pool one afternoon. She had not planned on being here for the hot weather so had no swimming suit. *I suppose it wouldn't have mattered if I had*, she told herself, watching the young people splashing in the water. She was wearing a pair of cotton shorts and a loose-fitting T-shirt, and her clothes seemed to fit tighter every day. She managed to purchase two new pairs of maternity pants when Cathy took a float plane to Vancouver one day. Alexis wouldn't have felt right asking--for it was a quick trip to visit Cathy's sick mother--but when Cathy offered to stop at a maternity store Alexis had jumped at the chance. Her blouses were not a problem yet, and the loose T-shirts she brought were the most comfortable. Fortunately, she would be going back to the harbor before she outgrew the new pants.

Crissy was faced with the same distress as her own jeans grew tighter, but one of the counselors who was close to Crissy's size, as well as a little overweight, was quick to come to the girl's aid. Alexis smiled at Crissy as the teen sat under one of the patio's large umbrellas writing a letter to a friend, and the red-headed teenager returned the smile. Just beyond Crissy, Alexis could see two groups of canoers rowing frantically to beat the rapids. Alexis was a little envious, for it had been several weeks since she had been on the water. Between Crissy and her camp responsibilities, there was little free time. She made a mental promise to try to go again soon.

Not once had she regretted her decision to stay. More and more every day she enjoyed her position at the camp, even if it meant doing laundry. And helping out in the kitchen allowed her to spend more time with her young charge, meet all of the campers, and watch the suppertime skits she liked so much. She was learning to prepare many new dishes as well. One of her favorites was oysters dipped in slightly beaten eggs, rolled in cracker crumbs and cooked to a crisp golden in a deep fat cooker. Lots of catsup along with a sauce made of mayonnaise, chili sauce and horseradish were served with crisp crackers. The oysters and crackers, topped off with homemade ice cream, had become a part of the traditional Friday night fish fry.

I'll bet Cliff would love oysters that way. Alexis's thoughts suddenly turned to her husband. She wondered what he must be doing at the moment--was he thinking of her at all? As the baby grew inside her, her love for Cliff grew stronger as well. She only hoped he wasn't still angry with her.

The 4th of July at Malibu turned out to be the highlight of Alexis's summer. Other staff had shared memories of other years, and Alexis had eagerly anticipated the event. Though she was a Canadian, she knew she would very much enjoy the celebration of the American Independence Day. Fireworks were brought in from Vancouver earlier in the week to be shot off over the water.

A customary supper of barbecued hamburgers, including potato salad, watermelon, lemonade, and cake was served outside in the barbecue pit. Paper plates and cups meant much less work for the dish pit crew. Skits that evening were to be set on a patriotic theme, followed by a good old-fashioned singalong. As soon as it became dark enough, the fireworks would begin.

"Our day of independence is July first," Alexis informed Crissy, who was from Washington State. Crissy was seated next to her eating a hamburger piled high with lettuce, tomatoes and pickles. "And it's called 'Canada Day.'"

"Oh, really? What do Canadians do to celebrate?" Crissy asked. Her eyes were bright with excitement as she awaited the evening's festivities.

"There's a great big parade in Vancouver, but we don't always get to go. July is a real busy time at the harbor."

"Do you set off fireworks over the water?" Crissy asked.

"Not on the first, but some of the tourists do on the fourth when they come up. Canadians don't set off fireworks for Canada Day, just Halloween."

"That's weird," Crissy said, wrinkling her nose.

Alexis laughed. "Spoken like a true teenager!" She reached over and affectionately rumpled Crissy's bright red hair.

* * *

Daily chapel, or "club" as Mr. Feldman called it, was one of the requirements of each staff member, unless duty required them to be elsewhere, and Alexis had faithfully followed the practice. One Thursday evening she slipped into an empty seat in the back row just as the speaker began. Because of helping clean up after supper, she had missed the song time, her favorite part of the evening routine.

Her mind wandered for a moment as she noted the camp's large German Shepherd lounging near the speaker's feet. No one seemed to mind. She smiled. Such a relaxed atmosphere was one thing she liked about the camp.

"'Thou has left thy first love,'" a deep male voice boomed, and Alexis jumped, startled, then blushed wondering if anyone had noticed. Was he speaking to her? She glanced up at the tall gentleman in surprise.

The speaker, a silver-haired man named Mr. Jeremiah, whom she had met earlier in the week, was gazing down at a Bible on the podium and appeared to be reading. "'Remember therefore from whence thou art fallen, and repent, and do the first works....'" He looked up from the open Bible to expound on the written text, but Alexis's thoughts carried her far away.

The words seemed to bore into her soul. "My first love." True, she had left Cliff, but had she abandoned God in the process?

As a child, she had accepted Christ rather matter-of-factly. The decision hadn't changed her life dramatically like some of the kids at Young Life whose testimonies she had heard. Alexis knew she was going to Heaven when she died, but other than that, her five-year-old heart had basically remained the same. She knew something was different, and she loved Jesus, but her day in, day out existence was as before. The initial excitement had worn off over time.

Similarly, her courtship and subsequent marriage to Cliff nearly three years ago had been a mountaintop experience. In the early days they were hungry for each other, always seeking the other out, anxious to see or touch or talk. Then the exhilaration wore off, and the daily routine became a familiar habit; life in the harbor was still pretty much like it had been in years past.

Alexis sat up in her seat, stunned. She had accused Cliff of taking her for granted, but had she taken him for granted as well?

Mr. Jeremiah continued. "God wants us to have that first love, that first excitement we had when first we accepted His holy gift, the gift of His son."

Tears blurred her eyes. Alexis wanted to have that old excitement back, but how? She listened intently to the rest of the sermon to see if Mr. Jeremiah gave an answer. When the service was over, Alexis quietly sought out one of the counselors. In a quiet room she rededicated her life to God, to do with as He chose.

A new enthusiasm filled her days, and Alexis eagerly awaited the time she would return to the harbor. Though anxious to tell Cliff about the baby, she was patiently waiting until she could share the news face to face. Having attributed many of her conflicting emotions to the early days of her pregnancy, she now seemed surrounded by a rosy glow and an abundance of good health. Crissy, on the other hand, spent many mornings in bed throwing up. Alexis was sympathetic but explained to Crissy that everyone handled pregnancy a little differently.

"Who'll help Frank in the kitchen if I'm here throwing up?" Crissy moaned one morning.

Alexis laughed. "Now don't you worry about that! Frank misses you, but he's getting along fine. Says to tell you the baby must be a boy if he's this ornery already!"

Crissy gave her a toothy grin.

* * *

Chapter Ten

Fall was just around the corner, and with it a chilly bite in the air. As the last set of campers boarded the Princess, Crissy and Alexis watched from the top deck. It seemed odd not to have a new group unboarding. The cruiser had arrived near empty, carrying only supplies and a few parents desiring a tour of the famous resort.

Alexis had to face the fact that it was time to leave for home. The camp no longer needed her, and there was no reason to linger. She had a life of her own waiting. A life which, finally, she was looking forward to.

She also had to figure out what to do with Crissy. At this point, there was absolutely no way she would send the girl home. All summer she and Crissy had prayed about her situation; they hoped that Kate and Charlie would let her stay with them. If not, Alexis reasoned, the resort had few guests during the year, why not let Crissy stay in one of the units?

Now if she could just sell her mother on the idea. Alexis was nervous as she called home. It had been almost four months. Would Cliff still be angry? Or would he just tell her to stay away? She knew she had toyed with his emotions, and he had implied that he would not be there when she returned. He had not written her once, not even on her birthday, and stopped texting after that first phone call.

No one answered Cliff's phone, so Alexis called her mother. "Mom, I'm coming home," she announced. "I'll be back sometime tomorrow afternoon."

"Oh, Honey, I'm so glad. We've all missed you. Do you have things settled in your mind?"

Alexis hesitated. "I--I think so. Much better, anyway. We can talk about it more when I see you. But Mom, I have to ask you something very important." As briefly as possible, she explained about Crissy, then held her breath.

"How awful for her," replied her mother thoughtfully. "Of course, we'll help, as long as we're not interfering. Have you spoken with her mother? Do you know for sure that she's telling the truth and not just trying to leave home?"

"I asked the same questions, Mom, and *yes*, I've talked to her mom. And she's had a pregnancy test. She's a neat teenager, I think you'll like her. There is definitely no hidden agenda here. Just an unwed mother who needs a home." She paused. "Her mother is in denial but wants what's best for Crissy. I think it's easier for her not to have Crissy around as a reminder." She paused, sending up a quick prayer. "What do you think?"

"Certainly, we'll take her," Kate said without hesitation. "I can fix up your old room, which is now filled with all of my own stuff!"

"Thanks, Mom, I knew you'd understand. We can talk more when I get home. Explain her to dad, too, will you? And Mom--I couldn't reach Cliff. Will you let him know? I have to get off the phone now and get packed up."

"Honey, Cliff--"

The telephone began to cut out. "Mom?"

"--work for--" her mother said.

"Mom, I can't hear you. You're breaking up. I'll see you tomorrow."

She let out her breath. Crissy, who was waiting anxiously outside the door, raised her eyebrows. "It's all set," Alexis announced, and gave the girl a hug. "Now, go pack your stuff." Crissy broke into a grin and scurried off to her cabin.

The next morning after breakfast, after many tearful goodbyes, Crissy and Alexis set out for Pender Harbor. Alexis, happy to go home but sad to leave Malibu, glanced up at the deck outside the dining room as she drove by. Besides Malibu being one of the most beautiful places she had ever seen, the weeks spent within its confines had been a time of growth. As the Seaswirl skimmed out the inlet, Alexis felt like she was leaving a tiny corner of her heart behind. She looked back over her shoulder and whispered, "Goodbye, Malibu!"

Crissy smiled with understanding and brushed a tear from her own cheek. The two were quiet for the first few miles, both pondering the changes in their lives over the last few weeks and the future that lay ahead. Alexis wondered how Cliff would take her announcement, fervently hoping she could spend some time with him alone before breaking the news. She thought of Crissy, and the many uncertainties that faced her in the next several months. Alexis hoped they would be able to find a good adoption lawyer nearby, but they would probably have to go to Vancouver.

"Alex, look!" Crissy suddenly shouted. "A house, out in the middle of nowhere." She pointed to the bank. The tiny white house, obviously unreachable except by plane or boat, sat near the edge of the water.

"Who in their right mind would live all the way out here?" Alexis wondered aloud. She had not noticed the house during her trip to Malibu in May, probably because of the early morning's darkness.

Crissy laughed. "Most likely a hermit. Or maybe an escaped criminal!"

Alexis smiled at the girl's imagination.

As they rounded the bend, Alexis noted a strange sound in the motor. "Crissy," she commanded, "shove the engine cover back away from the motor so I can listen to it."

"What's that?"

Alexis pointed to the large wooden shield. Crissy complacently removed the protective covering and Alexis listened. The motor was definitely not right. She had heard that sound before but could not determine what was out of place.

Suddenly, before she had time to give it much thought, the engine emitted a loud "pop!" then died.

Crissy's eyes widened. "Now what?" she asked, her face showing fear.

"Don't worry--I've seen this kind of thing before. Probably just needs a--" her voice trailed off as she turned off the key and went to assess the damage. Fiddling a bit, Alexis returned to the front of the boat and turned the key. Nothing.

Crissy waited, her large round eyes huge.

"We're going to have to use the little outboard motor," Alexis announced.

"Is that bad?"

"No, but I don't know if I have enough gas to get us the whole way home. All we can do is try. It partly depends on how bad the wind current is."

Crissy still looked so frightened that Alexis had to laugh. "Crissy, relax, it's okay! It's not like we're going to drown. Besides, boats are through here all the time-- it's likely we could get one of them to tow us."

The teenager visibly relaxed, and they started out once again. The Seaswirl moved at a snail's pace and Alexis wondered how long the small motor would hold out. The current grew stronger, and the wind blew against the boat, not with it. Unlike the many summer mornings Alexis had just allowed the boat to drift, today's weather threatened to storm. The elements could turn on them, fast. Even if weather conditions had been favorable, Alexis doubted that the gasoline would last all the way to Pender Harbor.

Trying not to let Crissy see her concern, she pondered what to do next. Still being closer to Malibu than to home, she considered calling someone there. Vainly she searched the water for another boat but found none. Just then rain began to pound on the bough of the boat, and Alexis shouted, "Crissy, help me get the hood up!" The two worked frantically trying to get the cover on as the boat rocked gently back and forth.

The craft putted along, and Alexis again considered their next move. In this weather, there was no way they could make it home. She switched on the marine radio and signaled for an operator, praying silently as she did so.

"Are we gonna be okay?" came Crissy's frightened voice.

Alexis had for a moment forgotten the girl's presence. "We'll be fine, Sweetie," she reassured her. "But I think we need more help than this little motor can give us. I'm calling for help. Pray, too, okay?"

After Alexis explained her predicament to the operator, a male voice crackled over the line. "What's your location?" he asked.

Alexis told him as best she could, then queried, "Do you tow?"

"Yes, I do."

"How far away are you?"

"From your description, you probably just passed my place," the voice responded. "I'm just around the bend in a small white house."

Alexis caught Crissy's eye and Crissy burst into a fit of giggles. Who better to live in the middle of nowhere than someone who towed stalled boats!

"Can you tow us to Pender Harbor?" Alexis asked, suppressing her own amusement. The man assured her that he could and said he would start out immediately.

"I should have asked him how much he charges," she commented to Crissy after hanging up.

Though the man's home was nearby, nearly a half hour passed before he reached them. Crissy waved eagerly at his boat as he approached. Fortunately, the rain had stopped for the moment and the wind had died down.

As the man stepped out of his towboat onto the Seaswirl, Alexis was never so glad to see anyone in her life. "Ma'am," he said politely, nodding his head. "I'll just tie this rope around the front of your boat and we'll be on our way." Alexis and Crissy watched curiously as the man expertly tied the two boats together.

"By the way, how much do you charge?" Alexis asked him just before he jumped back on board his own craft.

"Two hundred dollars," the man answered, without hesitation or apology.

Alexis gasped. "Okay," she managed to say. When he was out of earshot, she confided to Crissy, "If I'd known it was THAT much I might have just decided to paddle!"

Crissy giggled. "That *is* criminal!" she said jokingly, referring to her earlier comment about who would live in such a remote location.

Realistically, Alexis figured it was just as well that she hadn't asked his price before he had driven all the way out to tow them. The knowledge may have prompted her to try to make it on her own, and the boat would have taken hours longer and probably still needed towing.

The ride behind the larger boat was slow, but at least it was certain. Alexis's excitement heightened as they neared the harbor, and she could make out the docks and the buildings.

Autumn had arrived at the harbor in full splendor. The burnished red sweetgums contrasting with the brown pin-oaks and golden Maple trees painted a beautiful backdrop to which to return. At first glance, Alexis slowly sucked in her breath as her eyes took in the view. "Crissy, look!" she exclaimed. "There it is! That's Pender Harbor!"

Crissy grinned. In only minutes, the larger boat had pulled up beside the farthest dock. The driver jumped off the boat and walked back to disengage the rope.

Alexis gratefully paid him, grateful for the money she had earned over the past several months. She grimaced at the high figure but was thankful to be home safely. "Thanks," she told him. He touched the brim of his hat, pocketed the money, and pulled away from the dock.

Alexis started the little motor once again and pulled forward into her regular spot. After shutting off the motor, she instructed Crissy to loop the rope around the cleat and step onto the dock. Alexis gently allowed the boat to float alongside, then handed their bags to Crissy and jumped out. She and Crissy exchanged nervous glances, then turned to walk up the hill to her parents' home.

Alexis stood outside the house for a few moments. For the first time ever, she was afraid to open the door. A bit like the prodigal son felt, she imagined. "It's--it's been a while," she explained to Crissy. "I really don't know what to expect." Then, swinging the door open, she called out "Mom--Dad--"

A moment later, Alexis's fears were put to rest as her mother appeared in the hallway. "Oh, Honey, you're home!" Rushing toward her, she embraced Alexis in a tight hug. "And this must be Crissy," she said in her typically gracious manner, turning to the girl. "Welcome to Pender Harbor, dear."

Crissy gave her a shy smile, her bright red hair glistening in the early afternoon sunshine. "Thanks for letting me come," she said quietly.

After chatting for a few minutes, Alexis asked, "Where's Dad?"

"He's gone to town, honey. He'll be back before too long."

"Well." Alexis took a long, deep breath. "I wanted to get Crissy settled in. Can you show her to her room? I need to go find Cliff and face the music."

Her mother's face fell. "Oh, honey. That's what I was trying to tell you on the phone yesterday before we got disconnected."

"What?" Alexis braced herself for bad news. "He's not hurt or anything, is he?"

"No. But he--he went to Alaska to take a job."

"He *what*?"

"His aunt called and told him about a job. Some computer thing I don't understand, but we need to supplement our income somehow. With prices going up everywhere, the harbor can barely afford to support *one* family, let alone two!"

"Where in Alaska?" Alexis blinked hard to keep the tears from falling.

"I don't know exactly, but you can call his aunt. Cliff said--"

"What do you mean, you don't KNOW?" Alexis exploded. Crissy tactfully excused herself to find the bathroom.

"If you want to reach him, try his aunt's house," Kate suggested patiently, then her voice took on a sterner tone. "I'm not his mother, Alexis. I don't need to know where he is 24 hours a day. He's a grown man. And he's *your* husband, so don't be upset with me!"

Alexis blinked back tears. "I'm sorry, Mom," she said, her voice repentant. "Really. I'm just--I'm just so disappointed." Letting the tears fall, she accepted the sanctuary of her mother's arms, if only for a moment. "I was so hoping he'd be here, and we could--I could-- make things right again." She lifted her head to look into her mother's eyes.

"I understand, honey. It's all right. Does he know you're expecting?"

Alexis pulled back in surprise. "How did you know?"

Kate smiled. "Sweetie, I wasn't born in the dark ages. Have you looked in a mirror lately?" She chuckled. "I'm happy for you, dear. But back to my question--does he know?"

Alexis shook her head. "No, the baby will be a BIG surprise to him! Hopefully a pleasant one."

Crissy reappeared in the hallway. Saying goodbye to Crissy and excusing herself, Alexis carried her suitcase and hurried down the hill. She let herself into the cabin, feeling odd using a key when the door was so often left unlocked. Stepping inside, she slowly glanced around. *Definite signs of bachelorhood*, she thought ruefully. Living alone gracefully was definitely not one of Cliff's strong points. The trash can beside the sink was piled high with paper plates, plastic cartons and tin cans, and the dirt on the floor told her the place most likely hadn't been cleaned since before she left. Pulling open the fridge door, she found it bare except for a few condiments and cans of pop.

After making herself a fresh cup of tea, she set about trying to call Cliff's aunt, but no one answered. Disappointed, and weary from the trip from Malibu--made longer by the faulty motor--she dropped her head on the kitchen table and burst into tears.

After consoling herself with a good cry, she walked up to the big house to see how Crissy was getting along. "Hi," she said, tapping lightly on the door of her old room. "I didn't mean to abandon you. How's it going?"

Crissy impulsively gave her a hug. "I love your room! Look, your mom's even letting me use your old quilt--said you made it in sewing class in high school!"

Alexis, amused, fingered the old worn quilt and laughed. "She's right! But what she didn't tell you is that I got a very low grade on it because it's so crooked! Sitting patiently isn't one thing I'm very good at. Mom was proud of me anyway." Glancing around the room, she was filled with a sudden nostalgia. Though her mother had since moved in her own sewing supplies and more or less taken over, the sunny yellow wallpaper was still the same. The same bright print curtains framed the window overlooking the water, and the large stuffed teddy bear and other stuffed animals were still squashed together in a net strung from one corner of the room to the other.

Aware of Crissy watching her, she responded, "I'm glad you like it. I always did." She walked over to the window. "See, you can watch what everyone's doing." She was reminded of how she used to watch Cliff without him knowing it. As long as she was stuck inside folding laundry, she would dump it on her bed and watch the ongoings of the rest of the harbor while working. "Hmmm, I smell something good."

Crissy nodded. "Your mom's making cookies. Said now that September's here she has time to do things like that. And she knew you were coming home. She's making your favorite."

Alexis's eyes widened. "Not double-chocolate fudge?"

"Hmm hmmm."

Alexis was touched. She could tell that her mother was trying to soften the blow of Cliff being gone. Food was a healer of all wounds--especially double-chocolate fudge cookies! Her eyes filled with tears. Before Crissy had time to ask what was wrong, they heard the front door open, and Alexis fairly flew from the room and into her father's arms.

"Daddy!"

Charlie's face lit up and he set down the bag he'd been holding to give her a hug. Alexis couldn't hold the tears back.

"Was it that bad?" her father teased, wondering why the sudden emotions.

"No," she laughed, brushing the tears away and remembering Crissy's presence. "Daddy, this is Crissy."

"Well, HELLO!" he bellowed. The girl visibly shrank back, and Alexis laughed.

"Don't worry, Crissy, his bark is a whole lot worse than his bite. He's just a big teddy bear at heart."

Crissy, typically, giggled. "Pleased to meet you," she said shyly. "I--I think I'm going to go see if the cookies are done."

Alexis met her father's gaze. "Don't worry, she'll get over it. She's just a little afraid of men she doesn't know." She hesitated. "Daddy, I've got news. Crissy's not the only one who's pregnant."

She had never seen her father look so surprised. "I'm going to--that is, Cliff and I are going to have a baby!" she told him as he stood with his mouth open.

He gave her another hug. "Now, how did you manage that long distance?" he joked.

She hit him playfully on the arm. "I figure I'm about five months along. Cliff doesn't know yet."

Her father solemnly scratched his head. "Were you able to reach him?"

Alexis shook her head. "No, I'm going to try again tonight."

She made herself a sandwich, then went back to the cabin to give it a thorough cleaning. Returning to the big house for supper, she was happy to see Crissy, apron tied around her thick waist, bustling about in the kitchen as though it were her own.

Kate winked as Alexis entered the room. "Seems this girl knows her way around a kitchen."

"Yes, she does," Alexis admitted. "The camp's cook was very glad to have her help. What are you making, Crissy?"

"Beef stew. Your mom made it, I only cut up all the vegetables and browned the meat."

The two women burst out laughing. "Sounds to me like *you* made it," Alexis told her.

Over a supper of salad, stew, and homemade biscuits, Alexis and Crissy shared what they had been doing for the past couple of months. Crissy's shyness seemed to disappear as she told of the camp and the various activities. After washing up the supper dishes, Alexis headed to her cabin alone. The place seemed almost eerie without Cliff. Odd, how things could be exactly the same, but different. The dark water sloshing up against the dock seemed ominous and the moon cast a lonely glow through the curtains.

She once again phoned Cliff's aunt's home but got no answer. "Well, little one," she said, patting her belly. "You *do* have a father; we just have to find him!"

Alexis called the number the next day, and the day after that, to no avail. At the end of the first week, she mailed a short letter to his aunt's address.

She made doctors' appointments for both she and Crissy for the following week and used the getaway to take Crissy shopping for warm maternity clothes. Her mother had sent as much money as she could spare, and

Alexis was happy she was taking responsibility for her daughter. Alexis bought a few things for herself, and the two stopped on the way home and loaded up on groceries for both homes. Alexis was grateful that Crissy was along. Her heart was not in making a home for herself, without Cliff there to share it with her. Crissy bustled about, selecting boxes and bags off the shelves and crossing the items off the list. At the teenager's suggestion they bought a special bread as well as the sauce and cheese for making homemade pizza for supper.

Alexis slept restlessly and dreamed of Cliff often. That night after shopping, she had a vivid dream. His lips were gentle upon her face, his arms around her. He had just whispered something in her ear, and she was laughing....

The phone rang, and Alexis bolted straight up in bed. Grabbing the receiver, she shouted "Hello!"

"Sorry, wrong number," came the voice.

She slammed the phone down, annoyed at being disturbed. The luminous numbers told her it was only midnight--she had been asleep two hours. But the dream had been so real. If only she could go back to sleep and recapture it....

Another week went by, and still no word from Cliff. In the meantime, she tried to think of all the projects she could do *without* him. Opening the door to the spare bedroom, she pondered what changes would be needed to accommodate a baby. The room had become a catch-all, with unwanted clothing and other items, a coffeepot they no longer needed, and miscellaneous items from Cliff's bachelorhood days. Her old stenciling supplies and a sewing box were in one corner. What did people do with all this stuff? she wondered. The room was void of furniture except for her little desk which held her computer. Cliff had set the computer up so she could E-mail Jenny, but as the two got busier, writing each other became a thing of the past. *Maybe I should write Jenny today*, she mused. On the other hand, what could she say? *"Dear Jenny, Cliff and I are doing fine. We are currently separated, and he doesn't know I'm pregnant."* So much for that idea.

The room would need furniture for the baby, of course. When Cliff got home, they could go furniture shopping together. For a crib, a bassinet...a rocking chair would be nice.

Keeping her ideas in mind, she set to work. In the shed she managed to find four boxes. Rustling in the drawer for a marker, she wrote on the boxes: "TOSS", "GIVE AWAY", "FIX", and "KEEP (but move someplace else)". Starting through the closet, she pulled out each item and made a quick decision, tossing it into a box. Cliff's clothes she would leave for him to decide. Opening the shoeboxes on the shelves one by one, Alexis discovered treasures she had forgotten: her high school yearbooks; her grade-school papers; a diary from her teen years; her graduation tassel...several pink cocktail napkins with silver letters reading "Cliff and Alexis Forever".

At the sight of the tiny pink napkins, Alexis sat down on the floor and began to cry. She didn't even *feel* married at the moment. Pregnant, definitely. She had never felt so fat in all her life or had so many strange food cravings. Crissy's own tastes were a little more normal. She seemed to eat everything in sight but usually made healthy choices. Alexis sighed. If and when Cliff did come home, would he find a tired, fat, emotional wife? She wanted to be so much more for him.

Weary, she gave up the project temporarily, chose an uplifting Christian music station on TV, and ran a warm bubble bath. After soaking for half an hour, she felt like a new person. Feeling revived, she put on a fresh sweater and jeans and started in on the room again. By early evening the room was transformed. Her "GIVE AWAY" box was the fullest, and she was proud of herself for not being too sentimental. The following day she would take the box into town to the thrift shop, and maybe look around for furniture while she was there. By herself.

After the following week, Alexis once again considered her future. If Cliff had taken the job, surely he was putting money in their bank account. After all, he had a wife and child to support! Of course, he'd had no way of knowing that she was home. For all Cliff knew, his wife was off on escapades of her own, making her own money. But by now he should have received her letter and know that she was home and that she loved him. Was he staying away on purpose? She made a mental note to check their bank account later that evening.

Doubts tugged at her mind. Did Cliff still love her? Was he still angry? If only he would call, and she could get the answers she needed. She just needed to *talk* to him.

Alexis was finishing up some paperwork in the office one afternoon when the telephone rang. "Pender Harbor, may I help you?" she answered matter-of-factly.

There was a moment of silence, then-- "Alex?"

"Cliff, it's you! I've been trying to reach you for weeks." A rush of longing filled her, and she cradled the phone closer to her ear. "Where are you, how's your job? I tried to call your aunt but no one's home!"

"Whoa, slow down," Cliff laughed, but she could hear the tension in his voice. "I've been working long hours, and my aunt's been away. I'm staying in an Airbnb in a different town, and the reception's terrible. I'm calling you from someone's land line."

"Where exactly are you?"

They chatted for a few minutes, about the computer system he was setting up for a new business, how the harbor was getting along without him, and how cold Alaska was in September. But when it came to getting personal, Alexis was finding it difficult to break the ice.

"Cliff, I--"

"Yeah, Alex?"

"I--I don't know what to say. I needed that time away, and I can't explain why. But I still love you. I want to work things out. When are you coming home?"

"Probably not until Christmas--air fare is awfully expensive from Alaska. Are your mom and dad doing okay?"

"Yes, but--" Tears filled her eyes. She wanted him to ask about *her*, to give some sign that he even cared. How could she tell him about the baby over a long-distance phone call, without even being able to watch his eyes? It was not her idea of tactfully sharing the news.

"Cliff, I--I need to talk to you."

"I thought that's what we'd been doing," he responded.

She began to cry silently and breathed heavily into the phone.

"Alex--babe--are you all right?"

He had called her 'babe'. Maybe he wasn't mad, after all. "I'm okay," she told him. "Let me have your address. I'll write you a long letter."

"Okay. Then I've got to go, work's calling."

He gave her the information, then hung up, and Alexis clutched the phone tightly. Was Cliff so caught up in his world of business that he had forgotten all about her?

Slowly the truth dawned on Alexis. Was this how *he* had felt when she left him? For two weeks she'd had no word. Those weeks had been the longest in her entire life. Had the days without her been as long for Cliff? Before Cliff was her husband, he was her friend. How could she have done this to any friend?

She hugged her stomach and doubled over in tears.

That evening after returning to the cabin alone, Alexis sat down at the kitchen table with a cup of herb tea and carefully penned a letter. What made things even more depressing was the fact that today marked their third wedding anniversary. She had no idea if the date stood out in Cliff's mind as well--if so, he certainly had not mentioned it. She had given the letter much thought. It was time to bury her pride and just share her heart with him. She picked up her pen and began to write.

Dearest Cliff,

> *I am just now beginning to understand my own emotions and actions of the last few months. I hope and pray that you will read my letter with an open heart and mind and allow me back into your life.*

First, let me tell you that the months at Malibu were well spent. Ironically (and humbling!), the majority of my time was spent doing what I used to hate doing in the Harbor--laundry! But it was a tremendous help to the camp. Since the campers don't bring sleeping bags, all the beds must be re-made each week. I was especially needed when the cook became ill and was glad I had tested my culinary skills on you when we were first married!

Spiritually, I came closer to the Lord there more so than ever before in my life. I admit I have been trying to run things, and, perhaps, run AWAY from things. I don't totally understand what was going on, but I want very much for you to come home and for us to work things out. Also, I think that many of my strange emotions were due to changes within my own body. I have some very important news I would much prefer to tell you in person, but here goes--by mid-January there will be three of us! I've known for several months now. I hope you will be as happy as I am. I have been to the doctor, and he says I'm healthy and the baby is progressing well.

Cliff, my life is empty without you. Forgive me for treating your love so lightly. I understand now how hurt you must have been. Please write or call soon.

Ever yours,

Alex

She read the letter over carefully, then placed it in an envelope, copying down the address Cliff had given her. All she could do now was wait.

Now that she had reached Cliff, Alexis turned her attention to other matters. One thing had been weighing heavily on her mind, and she asked Crissy to come over one evening so they discuss it.

"Crissy, there's something we have to talk about," Alexis said, sitting on the couch and rubbing her hands nervously.

"Yes?" Crissy waited.

"I know you don't want to go to school, but--"

Crissy's eyes widened at the very mention of it. "No, Alexis, please. You promised."

Alexis held up a hand. "Now, just wait. I promised that you wouldn't have to *go* to school. What if school came to you?"

"What--what do you mean?"

"Mom knows of a woman who lives in Sechelt who used to be a teacher. They ran into each other at the grocery store last week, and the woman mentioned that she's so lonely now that her husband is gone. And she has a lot of time on her hands.

"So," Alexis went on, "Mom got this idea. What if she were to come over several hours a day and teach you? You know you have to pass the home schooling tests or the state will make you go to the regular school, Crissy."

Crissy had the beginning of a smile on her face. "There wouldn't be anything wrong with that," she responded, the idea slowly sinking in. "I just don't want to have to explain to other kids, ya know?"

Alexis nodded. "I know."

"Would we have to pay her?"

"We haven't worked that part out yet. Thought we'd better at least ask *you* first! Maybe we could work out a housekeeping arrangement or something."

Crissy's eyes widened. "Yeah--or maybe I could cook for her!"

Alexis laughed.

As it turned out, the arrangement was perfect for everyone. Alexis drove Crissy to the woman's house every weekday, where Crissy spent several hours daily under the woman's tutorage. In return, Crissy cooked a large noon meal for them both, usually with leftovers to freeze. The two became fast friends, and everyone hoped Crissy would be ready when test time arrived.

With Thanksgiving only a month away, Alexis began to get her hopes up. Certainly, Cliff would return home for the holiday! On the other hand, his aunt would probably be thrilled to have him for Thanksgiving, and he'd said that a flight home was awfully expensive.

Her hopes sank.

Kate, watching her from the sidelines, hid a growing concern for Alexis. They had not heard from Cliff, and life without a husband seemed to be taking its toll on her only child.

"Honey, I'm worried about you--you're not taking care of yourself," Kate told a bedraggled Alexis one morning. Her eyes bore dark shadows and her usually vibrant blonde hair was limp. "Have you been eating properly?"

Alexis shrugged. "I usually have some granola mid-morning along with my tea."

"What about fruit?"

"Sometimes. For supper I just make a sandwich or some soup."

Her mother frowned. "Alexis--why don't you come up to the house for supper for a while? At least until Cliff gets back."

"That's probably a good idea, Mom," Alexis answered gratefully. "At least when I was cooking for Cliff, I was taking care of me, too! It seems like so much work to fix something just for one person."

Her mother gave her an understanding smile. "I know, dear."

Alexis was grateful for the invitation. The dinners around the family table reminded her of happier times. She marveled at the young woman Crissy was becoming, growing in her relationship with God as the child inside her grew noticeably. Alexis sighed. She felt like there were *two* single mothers at the harbor, not just one. She knew the guests had begun to wonder what was going on, and several had not been shy about asking. If only Cliff were here, he would squelch all of their nasty rumors.

It had been a month since she had spoken with him. She received one letter, but it said nothing in response to hers, merely telling briefly of his work and enclosing a check for her to deposit. Why didn't he call? Surely, he must have received her own letter weeks ago. Now October, she was six months pregnant and still had not discussed it with Cliff! Hesitantly, she had a heart-to-heart talk with her mother one afternoon while Crissy tended the office.

"Mom, I've done everything I can think of," Alexis confided. "Why hasn't he called me?"

Kate shrugged. "Maybe he's afraid to face his own responsibilities. He was very hurt when you left, Alex.

To be truthful, I didn't know if he would make it through. He is very much in love with you, though sometimes men have different ways of showing it than we wish they did!" She chuckled. "He was devastated when he discovered you were gone, but as time went on, I think he also began to realize that he *had* let the comfortable, protected lifestyle here mean more to him than you. As his wife, it was only natural that *you* wanted to be the focal point of his life, and instead you had just become a part of the furnishings. Or at least you felt that way. Am I right?"

"Yes." Alexis was amazed at her mother's insight. "I wanted it to be like it used to be, just the two of us. Then, being pregnant and not knowing it, I think my body went crazy with all sorts of weird hormones. I feel fine now. Not restless like before. But I feel like there are *two* single mothers here in the harbor, not one. I just want Cliff back and for us to love and raise this child together." A tear slid down her cheek and she brushed it away.

"I know, honey," Kate nodded. "Shall we pray about it?"

In answer to their prayer, Cliff called that evening after Alexis had returned to the cabin. Alexis answered the phone nonchalantly, supposing it was her mother or Crissy. When Cliff's deep voice boomed through the phone, her heart leapt.

"Cliff! Did you get my letter?"

"No--did you write me one?"

Hot tears began to fall. He did not get her letter! It had explained everything, and he had not received it.

"Yes," she told him. "I wrote the same day I spoke with you before. How--how are you? I haven't heard from you." She hated to sound like a whiny wife but was frantic to talk to him.

"You got the check, didn't you?" he asked.

"Yes, but, I mean--you didn't answer my own letter, so I didn't know what to think. I can't understand why you didn't get it," she said, puzzled. "Have you been keeping busy?"

"I'll say. The one job is over with, but my partner and I have another computer system to install that will take us both to Sitka."

"Sitka!" Sitka was a million miles away, at least it seemed that way to her. Alexis shuddered. That most likely meant he would not be home for Thanksgiving.

"Yeah. Company pays for air fare, of course. But that means I won't be home for a while. How are you doing?"

"Oh, Cliff." She pushed her pride aside and let the words roll over her tongue. "I love you, I need you, and I want you." There, she had said it. All the cards were on the table. On hearing the truth, would he reject her still?

The line was silent, so she continued. "Cliff, I--will you forgive me for treating your love so lightly?"

Those seemed to be the words Cliff was waiting to hear. "You know I will, sweetheart. Will you forgive me for being a jerk on the phone when you were at Malibu?"

She laughed. "You weren't a jerk. You were just hurt, with good reason. I--I understand now what I was going through. I just--I just want us to be together. When can you come home?"

"Well, honey, I've still got a job to do here. You know we need the money. In fact, I'll be sending you another check just before leaving for Sitka."

"I don't want the money, Cliff, I want *you*. Won't you be home for Thanksgiving?"

"No, but Christmas for sure. In fact--"

"Cliff, there's something I've got to tell you!" Alexis practically burst with the news.

"What is it, Hon?"

"I--I'm...pregnant!"

The line was silent, and Alexis wished with all her heart that she could see his reaction.

"You're what?"

"Cliff, we're going to have a baby!"

Again, there was silence, and Alexis was aware only of her own breathing and the dripping of the kitchen faucet. "Cliff, are you there?"

"Yeah, I--I'm a little in shock, I guess."

Tears smarted her eyes. "Is that all you have to say?"

"Well, you must admit it's kind of a surprise. How long have you known?"

"Since my second month at Malibu, but I wanted to tell you in person. Actually, learning about Crissy's situation helped me to understand my own."

"Who's Crissy?"

"She--oh, Cliff, can't you please come home! It seems ridiculous to be telling you all of this on the phone. Why didn't you get my letter?"

"I have no idea. Did you use the address I gave you?"

"Yes."

"Zip code and all?"

"I think so. Just a minute." She fumbled on her desk for the paper on which she had written the address and read it back to him.

"Oh, babe--you put 'AL'?"

"Yes, for Alaska."

"'AL' is for Alabama. 'AK' is for Alaska. That's probably why I didn't get it."

"Oh. I'm sorry."

"No, *I'm* sorry," Cliff told her. "I thought you didn't care enough to write me. From this far away, Alex, I have no way of knowing what's going on in your head. I still remember the wife who left me in May."

"I know."

"And babe--"

"Yes, Cliff?"

"I love you. And I'm happy about the baby, really. I'm just surprised, that's all. Can you hang in there 'til Christmas? Then I'll be home for good. I promise."

"Okay," she said reluctantly. "Cliff, I love you, too. Bye." She hugged the phone to her heart. Feeling better, she hung up and called her mother.

* * *

Part of their harbor tradition was to stay home on Thanksgiving Day and let the townsfolk come calling. The big house was a popular meeting place. Alexis attributed part of that popularity to her mother's famous pecan pies, which the guests had grown to expect.

Alexis wondered if this year would be any different. Somehow, she couldn't get excited about the holidays--not without Cliff. She tried to keep too busy to think about it and poured her time and energy into preparing the guest rooms for company. The harbor was a favorite holiday spot for a certain opulent group from Vancouver, who wearied of the usual Thanksgiving traditions. Early in the week, she and Crissy cleaned each room to be used by the group. They spent the better part of a day making pinecone wreaths to decorate with, something Crissy had learned in an art class.

One afternoon, from Alexis's position cleaning a room above the office, she saw a dark blue car pull up, and her heart leaped. Cliff! Maybe he had come after all! She tore out of the room and down the stairs, only to be greeted by a family of five who needed lodging for the night. Alexis blinked back tears and booked them a room.

That evening she pulled out the special Thanksgiving card she had purchased especially for Cliff. She penned a quick letter, telling how busy she had been and how much she missed him. "Of all the things I have to be thankful for," she wrote, "I'm especially thankful for YOU. God has given me a new love for you, Cliff. All of us will miss you at Thanksgiving, but I'm freezing a whole pecan pie for your first night home!"

The three women spent the day before Thanksgiving baking pies. Crissy had also baked and decorated tray after tray of turkey-shaped sugar cookies. She insisted they were a favorite with children. Kate and Charlie were grateful for Crissy and the help she was to them and delighted in all of her creative ways. She had found her niche beside Alexis's mother, helping to prepare many of Kate's favorite dishes. Kate was an expert cook and Crissy a quick and eager learner. Crissy thrived on the attention the older woman was giving her, which seemed to make up for what she had missed from her own mother. Charlie took a special liking to her as well. Though she was shy with him at first, a mutual fancy for a good game of chess brought Crissy out of her shell. Charlie was thrilled to take on someone with the patience to try to outscheme him, and in Crissy he had met his match.

On Thanksgiving morning, Alexis rose early and walked up the hill to help her mother. Though the house would be filled with many hungry eaters, the meal would actually be quite simple to prepare. The turkey would go in the oven early, so it could be carved just after the guests arrived around two. Alexis had made an ambrosia cream salad, one of her own favorites. Her mother was baking homemade rolls along with all of the standard dishes she prepared every year--green bean casserole, cranberry relish, a vegetable tray, sweet potatoes with marshmallows, stuffing with mushrooms.

Alexis carried in her arms the large autumn arrangement Cliff had wired to her the day before. The flowers, comprised mostly of chrysanthemums and carnations, enhanced with autumn leaves, would make a lovely centerpiece for the table.

One of Alexis's favorite things about Thanksgiving was exactly that--giving thanks. Ever since she was a child each member of the family had his or her chance to say what they were thankful for. This year, though Crissy and several guests were in attendance, Kate kept up the tradition. One of the older male guests was grateful for good health, and his wife for loving friends. Charlie was especially thankful for his wife, he told everyone while winking at her. Kate said she had too many blessings to name, but she named a few anyway. Alexis was grateful for God's love and God's peace. And for her family. And Cliff.

Crissy's turn was last. She had been very quiet while the others were speaking. When Kate nodded to her, she lowered her head for a moment. Then she began softly, "I think I have more to be thankful for this year than ever before," she told everyone. "I have a new family--at least for a while--who loves me. I've never, ever lived in a house this beautiful or had so much good food to eat." She glanced over at Alexis. "I'm thankful for Alexis, and how she's helping me. And," here she hesitated. "And I don't have to be afraid anymore."

Alexis blinked back a tear while another female guest reached over and clasped Crissy's hand. Charlie closed the thanksgiving by offering thanks to God Himself.

* * *

Chapter Eleven

Snow falling on Pender Harbor was one of the most beautiful spectacles Alexis had ever seen. This year it was even more so, marred only by Cliff not being there to see it with her. He had only seen the Harbor several times in December, and Alexis longed to share it with him.

"We'll show him soon, little one," she told her unborn child, patting her well-rounded stomach.

Crissy's major dilemma had not been in locating a home for her baby. That part had been easy, as the adoption agency recommended to them by their lawyer offered plenty of loving couples wishing to adopt. The problem was where Crissy would go after giving birth. Kate, disgusted at the apparent lack of concern by Crissy's mother, had called the woman and asked her to come for a visit so they could all talk.

As for the rape itself, one night Kate and Alexis sat up late talking with Crissy about whether or not to take her stepfather to court.

"Would it mean he'd go to jail?" Crissy had asked.

"Hopefully yes," Kate told her, "but remember, too, that testifying in court can be a very trying experience. Often defense attorneys try to smear the girl's reputation--"

"But I haven't done anything!" Crissy protested.

"--and try to make it seem like she'd done something to bring it on herself--"

"But I didn't!"

"I know that, honey, I'm just telling you. It's totally your decision whether or not to prosecute. I'm just warning you that it can be emotionally draining, not to mention embarrassing. Everything that happened you would have to go over and over again on the witness stand."

Crissy broke into tears. "And what about my mom?"

"What do you mean?"

"How can I send my mother's husband to jail?"

Kate and Alexis exchanged glances. "Just pray about it," Kate told her. "This family will support you no matter what you decide."

"What about legal expenses?" Crissy asked.

"Well, maybe we could work out something with Mr. Sams, the lawyer who told you about the adoption agency. Or sometimes if a person can't afford a lawyer, there are county services to help."

They had not spoken further of it since. The day Crissy's mother was to arrive, Crissy was filled with anxiety. She refused to eat breakfast until Kate gently nudged her, reminding her of the baby's health. Crissy sat at the kitchen table across from Kate and slowly ate a container of yogurt and a piece of toast. "I just don't know about this," she moaned to Kate. "You don't know my mother! She has a way of making trouble for everyone. And what if she brings *him* along?" she asked, her eyes watering.

"Now Crissy dear, she's not bringing your stepfather," Kate assured her. "She's coming all by herself. And she can't be all *that* bad if she has such a lovely daughter, can she?"

Crissy attempted a smile.

Kate continued. "We'll all have a real nice talk about your future and what's best for you, and hopefully come up with a plan. Okay?"

"Okay," Crissy agreed, wiping her nose.

By the time Alexis arrived at the house, Crissy had done two loads of laundry, vacuumed the house, and baked a batch of cookies. "I like to keep busy when I'm nervous," she had told Kate, and asked if there was anything Kate wanted her to do. Kate had just vacuumed the day before but kept silent at Crissy's ambitions.

"Hmmm, the kid's good," Alexis teased after tasting a fresh cookie. Crissy grinned and came over to her for a hug. Just then they heard the crunch of tires in the driveway and Crissy's head jerked back. The kitchen timer went off, and Kate said calmly, "Crissy honey, why don't you take the cookies out of the oven while I go get to know your mother a little."

Crissy silently nodded, and Alexis followed her mother into the living room. The women had decided it best for Charlie to be "elsewhere" until later. His temper tended to get the best of him at times, and Kate and Alexis needed a good heart-to-heart talk with Crissy's mother without letting their emotions get out of control.

Kate opened the door. The woman on the doorstep made a pitiful sight, and Alexis instantly felt sorry for her. Her clothing had seen better days, and her pale blue eyes looked tired and a little afraid.

Kate graciously invited her in and offered to take her coat. The woman's shoulder-length dark hair fell limply around her shoulders, and her eyes darted nervously around the room. She removed her obviously worn overcoat to reveal an even more worn house dress. Kate accepted her coat, handing it to Alexis.

"I'm Kate, and this is my daughter Alexis," she told her.

The woman nodded at Alexis. "Pleased to meet you. I'm Francine."

"Please sit down. Would you care for a cup of coffee?" Kate asked. "Crissy just made cookies, too."

"Crissy always did make good cookies," the woman replied, her face softening. "A cup of coffee would be real nice."

Alexis, taking her cue, hung the coat up in the hall closet, then entered the kitchen. Crissy was slowly taking up the cookies, one by one, and placing them on the counter. "How about a few of those for our meeting?" Alexis suggested, pouring three cups of coffee from the pot.

Silently Crissy placed a dozen or so cookies on a plate and carried them into the living room. Alexis was right behind her with three cups of coffee on a tray.

"Crissy, honey," said her mother, standing suddenly.

Crissy looked embarrassed. "Hello, Mother."

The woman seemed to want a hug, but Crissy did not offer one. Instead, she sat in a chair at the far end of the room and Alexis took a seat on the couch. After several minutes of surface conversation, the room fell silent.

"Well..." Kate began. "I guess we should get down to talking about what really matters. First, I want to thank you for letting Crissy stay with us. She's been a real joy to us--a good cook, too, I might add!"

Crissy, a little more relaxed by now, grinned appreciatively at her. Alexis marveled that her mother was turning this around to make it look like the woman was doing *them* a favor, not the other way around.

"She's a lovely child--full of sparkle and laughter, in spite of the unpleasant situation she's found herself in," Kate continued. "I think she's been happy here. It's a good arrangement for everyone."

"What about the baby?" Francine suddenly asked.

Crissy piped up. "I've decided to give the baby away, Mother."

Francine nodded but made no comment.

"The lawyer told us about an adoption agency that is being very helpful," Kate explained. "Crissy actually gets to choose who adopts her baby. Being a Christian, she naturally wants a Christian couple."

Francine's face had turned white. "Lawyer?" she asked.

"Yes, a family friend of ours that goes to our church."

"What about--what about the--"

"If you're worried about me ruining George's reputation, don't be, Mother," Crissy said coldly. Her hands were shaking and her voice quivery as she continued. "I've decided not to take him to court."

Francine's eyes filled with tears, and she began to sob. "Oh, honey, I'm so sorry. So sorry."

Crissy's own eyes filled but she didn't move from her chair. Instead, she said softly, "So am I, Mother. I can't say I've forgiven him, but I don't hate him anymore. In time I know God will help me to forgive." She rose from where she was sitting and walked over to her mother, placing her arms around her. The two both cried for several minutes as Kate and Alexis sat silently by.

Crissy sat down beside her mother on the couch. "At least something good has come of all this," she told her mother. "I've met some really wonderful people. The Ryans have been great to me. Charlie--that's Mr. Ryan--and I play chess a lot, and he eats anything I cook."

Her mother sniffed and broke into a smile.

"There's a lady in town schooling me," Crissy continued, "so I'll be able to pass the tests okay. I didn't want to go to a regular school where kids might tease me, and I'd have to explain everything. Or worse--" her voice grew very quiet "they might think I was *that* kind of a girl." She stared at her lap.

Her mother nodded.

"My husband and I have been talking," Kate broke in. "We'd like for Crissy to stay with us as long as she wants to."

Surprised, Crissy's head popped up.

"That might be until just after the baby's born, or until summer comes, or until she's an old lady." Kate's voice was teasing, but her words were serious. "We consider it a blessing to have her."

Crissy looked over at her mother, waiting for an answer.

"Well, she can't come home, that's for sure, not the way things are...." Her voice trailed off. "I--for a while things were bad with George and me, after I learned what he done and all. But he *is* my husband. And I don't know what I'd do if he were in jail. We barely make ends meet as it is."

Just then they heard heavy footsteps on the porch. The front door opened, and Charlie entered the room. Surprising them all, Crissy got up and flung her arms around him.

Embarrassed, Charlie nodded to the newcomer in introduction. "Charles Ryan," he told her. "You must be Crissy's mother."

By early evening, Crissy's mother was on her way back home. She had fully agreed with the Ryans' plans, and Crissy, though happy to be staying at the harbor, was emotionally exhausted and decided to go to bed early. Charlie had fallen asleep in his chair, and Kate and Alexis were putting away the supper dishes and talking over the day's events.

"It will be almost like having another daughter," Kate confided in Alexis that evening when they were alone. "Alexis, did you know I had three miscarriages before I became pregnant with you?" Kate had a faraway look in her eyes.

Alexis was shocked. "No, Mom, I had no idea. I know you had me when you were thirty-eight, but I just figured I was a summer surprise!"

Kate smiled. "Your dad and I wanted children for a long time," she said softly. "But it just seemed it wasn't God's choice for us. When I got pregnant with you, I was still mourning a little boy I'd lost at two months."

Alexis laid a hand on her mother's arm.

Kate continued. "I was still so 'out of it', and my system was so out of whack by all the emotional upheaval that I hardly realized I was pregnant. By the time I figured it out, I was afraid to believe it was true." She paused. "I guess it wasn't until you were born that I actually believed you were here to stay!"

Alexis gave her a warm smile. "Mom, I appreciate so much you taking Crissy. I feel a real...kinship with her. She's so vulnerable. And I feel so bad about her home situation. It *is* almost like having a little sister."

Kate wholeheartedly agreed. "Your dad and I used to regret that you didn't have a brother or sister. For your sake, more than anything." She smiled wistfully. "But then, I guess you never were lonely around here, were you?"

Alexis raised her eyebrows and shook her head vigorously.

One evening in mid-December, Cliff called and said he was on his way home. Ecstatic, Alexis ran up the hill to tell her folks. Adding to her excitement, the ultrasound had confirmed that her baby was a girl.

"Did you tell Cliff about the baby?" Kate asked her.

"You mean that it's a girl? No. I wanted to keep it a surprise."

"Sweetheart," Charlie drawled. "Don't you think Cliff has had enough surprises lately?" He raised one eyebrow at her.

Kate and Alexis broke out into spontaneous laughter.

"Oh Daddy, you know how I am about surprises!" Alexis cajoled. "Besides, he'll know soon enough. Only another week or so before he's home!"

Two days later Alexis bought yards and yards of pink ribbon material at the fabric store in Sechelt. She was glad to have taken Crissy along, for Crissy was thrilled with all of the colored fabric, ribbons, buttons, and crafts in the little shop. While Alexis was paying for her purchase, Crissy carefully selected a needlepoint kit. With her baby just days away, her activities were limited, and she was bored with television and puzzles.

As soon as they arrived home, Alexis cut the long ribbon to numerous ribbons several inches long. She pulled a stepstool out under the tree and tied a pink ribbon on all of the branches she could reach. The branches being otherwise bare, the ribbons seemed a ridiculous adornment in contrast with all of the red and green Christmas decor in the harbor, but Alexis was determined to do it for Cliff.

"Should you be doing that?" Crissy asked as she walked by, worried Alexis would fall.

"Sure. I used to climb these trees when I was a kid. I--"

She stopped abruptly as Crissy's face turned pale.

"Crissy--are you okay?"

"Alexis, I--I think I'm in labor!"

Trying to be calm, Alexis walked the teenager back up to the house. They had prepared for this, she told herself. Crissy's bag was packed and waiting in her room; Alexis would drive her to the hospital and be her birthing coach, staying with her until the baby was born. What worried them wasn't the birth, but the emotional impact afterwards of giving the baby away, and the pain involved a month later when Alexis's own daughter was born. Would Crissy then have second thoughts?

"Mom!" Alexis yelled, and Kate, sensing something was wrong, hurried out from the kitchen where she had just taken a tray of cookies from the oven. "Crissy's having labor pains!"

Calmly, Kate asked, "How long have you been having them?"

"I noticed a little pain right after lunch," Crissy responded, "but I thought it was the spaghetti!"

"How far apart are they?"

"Hmmmm, five or ten minutes, I'm not sure."

Kate smiled knowingly. "We've got a while to wait. Why don't I fix us all a cup of tea? Crissy, dear, tell me when the next one comes, and we'll start timing them."

Crissy nodded. Alexis was still fidgeting restlessly near the door. "Honey, relax," Kate told her. "Until the pains are closer, nothing's going to happen."

"Okay, Mom. You're right." Alexis was certain she would be calmer at having her own baby. But Crissy was so young, and she wanted to somehow shield her from the pain she would face in the next few hours.

Kate headed for the kitchen and returned several minutes later with three cups of tea on a tray. Crissy had found an easy chair and was working on her needlepoint while Alexis turned on the television and began flipping channels.

"What's all this?" Charlie asked, suddenly appearing from outside. He removed his boots, one by one, setting him by the door, and wiped his brow.

"Crissy's in labor," Alexis informed him. "Just started."

"Well, that gives us just about enough time for a game of chess then, doesn't it?" he boomed in his loud voice. "How 'bout it, Crissy?"

Everyone laughed. Leave it to Charlie to calm three women down. Just then Crissy's hand went to her stomach, and she took a long, deep breath. Kate noted the time and wrote in down on a piece of paper. Charlie, calm as ever, methodically set up the chess board and pieces, then waited until Crissy was ready.

While Alexis sipped her tea, Kate passed a plate of cookies around. Alexis had turned the television off and was browsing through a magazine. Except for an occasional grunt from Charlie as he contemplated his next move, the room was quiet. Kate timed each pain and commented that they were getting closer together.

"I'm going to the cabin for my purse," said Alexis. "I'll call her doctor while I'm there."

Kate nodded. She grabbed Crissy's overnight bag from the bedroom and set it next to the front door.

"The doctor will meet us at the hospital," Alexis announced, entering the house minutes later with her bag slung over her shoulder. "Crissy, you ready?"

Crissy's eyes were apprehensive. "I guess so." She looked over at Charlie.

"Now little one, it'll be just fine," Charlie told her gruffly, pushing his chair back from the dining room table and in his haste knocking it over. He hurried around to assist Crissy out to the car. "A young thing like you, it'll be over in no time."

"We'll be praying for you, honey," Kate told her gently, giving her a motherly hug. Crissy's eyes brimmed. Silently, she picked up her bag and walked slowly to the car.

"Mom," Alexis said quietly after Crissy had gone outside. "Call the lawyer, will you? The adoptive parents need to be notified."

At the hospital Alexis calmly checked Crissy in, soothing her with quiet encouragement. She filled out the necessary papers as best she could and waited with Crissy until she was wheeled into a room. The lawyer arrived shortly thereafter with a sheath full of legal documents to be signed. He explained that the adoptive parents had been called and would be along soon to be a part of the hospital experience.

When the two women were alone again, Alexis asked, "How are you doing, hon? I mean, about giving the baby up?"

Crissy sighed. "Well, in some ways I don't even want to hold it. Ya know? I know I'll fall, hard. That's what everyone says. But I also think that if I don't ever see or hold my baby, I'll feel like it died."

Alexis agreed.

"Oooh!" Crissy grabbed her mid-section in pain. "That one was a little worse!"

After the pain had subsided, Alexis pushed the issue further. "So, do you want to hold the baby afterward? Let me know now, before it's born, because in all of the emotional upheaval afterward it won't be a good time to make a decision."

Crissy's tear-filled eyes met hers. "Yes. Just once. Alone."

Alexis nodded. "Done."

For the next four hours Alexis was a coach and an encourager. She stood ready with ice chips when Crissy got thirsty and prepared a cool cloth for her brow. At six-thirty the next morning, Crissy gave birth to a healthy baby boy.

As soon as possible after the birth, Alexis practically demanded that everyone leave Crissy and the baby alone. The lawyer, worried that Crissy would change her mind, was hesitant.

"Legally, she has a year to change her mind anyway," Alexis reminded him with a glare. "Look, she needs this. Give her this."

After everyone left the room, Crissy sat up in bed holding her baby and speaking softly to him. After a few minutes she called to Alexis and asked her to bring in the adoptive parents.

In a way that touched all of their hearts, Crissy handed the baby to the mother with tears in her eyes. "I prayed for a Christian family for my baby," she told them. "God answered that prayer in you two. I'm entrusting him into your care. Give him all the love and nurturing that I would have if I could. If things had been different."

She continued. "And don't worry about me changing my mind. He's not mine anymore--he's yours. God wants me to move ahead with my life and not look back. The next time I have a baby, it's going to be with my future husband. When the right time comes."

By now the adoptive mother was in tears, and, thanking Crissy, she tenderly cradled the baby boy in her arms as though he would break. "We've wanted a child for years," she told Crissy. Her husband gazed lovingly down at the baby, and everyone was silent for a few minutes.

"We'd better let you rest now," said the woman. "We'll be back tonight to take the baby home. And Crissy, dear--again, thank you."

"You did good, kid," Alexis told Crissy when they were alone. She stroked Crissy's hot, damp forehead with her hand. "I'm very proud of you. Now get some sleep. I'll be back later on. The doctor says you can go home tonight."

"Thanks for being my coach, Alexis. I couldn't have done it without you." Crissy gave her a tired smile, then closed her eyes.

Alexis was exhausted. But before leaving the hospital for home, she stopped by the hospital's florist shop and ordered a flower arrangement, asking that it be delivered right away to Crissy's room.

Returning to the harbor, she was too tired to notice the dark blue Blazer parked near the office. She only knew that she needed to find a bed for at least a few hours.

Opening the front door of the cabin, Alexis was surprised to find it unlocked. She gasped. A vase filled with a dozen red roses sat on the kitchen table! Confused, Alexis frowned. The flowers were supposed to go to Crissy, not her. And how--

All of her questions were answered when she heard a sound from behind her and turned.

"Cliff!"

In an instant she was in his arms.

* * *

Chapter Twelve

For the next few days, the couple walked around like newlyweds, holding hands and laughing over nothing. Life was as Alexis had hoped it could be. Cliff seemed happy about the baby, though he teased her about there being "more of her to love". Together they scoured baby books for just the right name.

"Amanda," Alexis contributed.

"Melissa," Cliff countered.

"Robin," Alexis offered.

Cliff broke into a wide grin. "Alex, think about it. Robin's a pretty name, but it would sound awfully funny with the last name of 'Hunter', now, wouldn't it?"

Alexis sighed. "Somehow I knew it was a mistake not to marry Doug Pender when I had the chance." She ducked as Cliff threw a couch pillow at her.

Alexis was well aware that Cliff's affection was guarded. He seemed to be watching her, as though he were certain she would slip into old habits of complaining and restlessness. And that made her all the more determined not to.

From Cliff's point of view, he was amazed and pleasantly surprised at the woman his wife had become. While her figure was not what it had been, her face held a rosy glow he had never seen before. There was a spring to her step and a sparkle in her eye that replaced the old defiant look of rebellion. He liked what he saw. He just hoped it lasted.

A week-and-a-half before Christmas the two of them, along with Charlie and Crissy, ventured into the woods to seek the perfect Christmas trees for the two households. Kate waved them off, assuring them she needed to get some baking done while they were gone. After much tromping about in the woods, they agreed on the two trees to take home. The ten-foot spruce they returned with was a real find for the big house. A shorter, bushier tree would be perfect for the front window of the cabin.

Admiring the final touches of tree-trimming the week before Christmas, Cliff stood back to give it a once-over. Alexis was standing nearby, and as his gaze landed on her, he fell in love with her all over again. His heart swelled at the love in her eyes when she noticed him watching.

One night the two of them had a heart-to-heart talk long into the night. "I was afraid of coming home to a selfish, possessive woman and wishing I had just stayed put!" Cliff confessed.

Alexis listened sympathetically, then shared her own feelings. "I was afraid you had given up completely and that things would never be the same again. It's as though Malibu gave me a second chance to be your wife," she told him.

"Just don't ever leave me again," he said huskily. "I couldn't bear it." Then he took her tenderly in his arms, and the last thing on her mind was leaving.

Christmas was fast approaching, as was, Alexis remembered almost too late, Crissy's birthday. After discussing it with the family, they all determined to make this her best birthday ever. The usually buoyant teenager had been depressed lately, and a letter from home several days before her birthday had sent her to her room in tears. Crissy's mother sent regular letters, and a little money for her support, but it was clear that the Ryans' decision to take Crissy was the best thing that could have happened to her. In her latest letter, she told Crissy that she was glad Crissy wouldn't be pressing charges; George had expressed remorse at what he had done, and she had no desire for her husband to spend the better part of his life in prison. Besides, she had added, George had told her that Crissy had "come on to him" from the first.

"That's a flat-out lie!" Cliff blurted after finding out.

"I know," Alexis nodded. "It's totally untrue. Crissy is--was--one of the most sweet and naive teenage girls I've ever met. Unfortunately, she's no longer so naive, but I hope all of this doesn't change her sweet nature." She paused, "I feel sorry for Crissy's mother. Like Mom says, in many ways, she's a victim, too. What choice does she have? If she chooses *not* to believe him, it's more or less admitting her husband is a rapist. What woman wants to believe that? This way, in her eyes, he just 'gave in to temptation'."

Cliff shook his head in disgust.

"I'm not defending her," Alexis continued. "I'm just glad Crissy has us, and Mom and Dad. See, at least that's one good thing that came out of me leaving!"

Cliff reached over and squeezed her hand. "I guess sometimes God uses us in spite of ourselves, doesn't He?" he admitted.

Alexis nodded, then jumped as the baby kicked inside her, and they both laughed.

The birthday celebration was held a few days before Christmas at the big house. Kate had prepared Crissy's favorite dinner of fried chicken, biscuits, mashed potatoes and gravy. After supper the five of them gathered in the living room so Crissy could open her gifts. Alexis and Cliff were pooling their resources with Kate and Charlie to buy Crissy a whole new wardrobe. Fortunately, the girl had simple tastes, mostly jeans and shirts. They all agreed that since Crissy would soon be able to lay aside her maternity clothes, it was high time for a change.

The small box Alexis wrapped earlier in the day held a tiny cross necklace. "Crissy *still* needs something to open," she had insisted. "It's just not a birthday without a present to unwrap!"

Crissy loved the necklace, and upon looking at the sizeable amount on the VISA gift card for her shopping spree, her eyes misted. "You're much too good to me," she told her new family. "I love you all so much." She hugged them each in turn, then whispered to Alexis, "I don't know what I would have done if you hadn't listened to me that day in the laundry room."

Alexis's eyes filled with tears, and she was reminded of her earlier conversation with Cliff. God *did* bring good things, even out of bad circumstances or poor choices.

While the women dabbed at their eyes, Charlie was getting impatient. "Bring on the cake!" he shouted.

In response Crissy threw her arms around him and his own eyes watered. "Happy birthday, sweetheart," he told her gruffly.

Kate disappeared into the kitchen and returned with a large chocolate cake with pink icing. "Sweet sixteen," the letters spelled out. Crissy 'ooohed' with delight and cut pieces for everyone, while Alexis added a generous portion of peppermint ice cream to each bowl.

"Remember my sixteenth birthday?" Alexis whispered to Cliff, fondly remembering the dinner at Fisherman's Inn, the rose in a crystal vase, the tackle box...and the goodnight kiss. Cliff kissed her cheek in response.

The next morning, Alexis took Crissy on a shopping trip to Vancouver. After all that had happened, the excursion was a much-needed break for both of them. The two made a day of it, eating breakfast on the ferry and planning what gifts to buy for the family. In all the excitement of the past few weeks, Alexis had done very little shopping.

Pausing before a rack of sweaters priced half-off, Alexis scrutinized one and called to Crissy. "Look-- wouldn't this be great on Mom?" The sweater, a multi- colored affair featuring yellow scarecrows and a farm scene, was just the type of thing Kate liked and would be perfect for those chilly mornings around the grounds. Crissy agreed. They found a sweater for Crissy as well, then scoured the sale tables in the back and were delighted to find low prices on blue jeans. By the end of the day, their arms loaded with packages, they dropped, exhausted, into a coffee shop just outside the ferry terminal.

"What'd you buy Cliff for Christmas?" Crissy asked after ordering a cup of hot chocolate.

"Well, the baby is all we can really afford," Alexis admitted, "but I know he's been wanting a cordless tool set for a long time, so I've been saving. That's one thing Dad's picking up for me since I know absolutely nothing about tools!" The two laughed. "Look what I got Dad, though!" She withdrew a small sack from a larger bag and pulled out a flashlight. "See, it wraps around a pole or whatever--so you don't always have to hold onto it!"

Crissy, too, was excited about her purchases. She managed to find Kate a heart pendant which they both agreed would look lovely with the new sweater Alexis was giving her. Crissy's gift to Alexis was a well-kept secret; cologne for Cliff and Charlie completed her gift-giving buys. Crissy was most excited about her own new clothes. Besides the jeans and shirts, underwear and a pair of new shoes, they made one final purchase of a kelly-green dress with black buttons, which Crissy could wear to church and other semi-formal gatherings. Because of its high waist, she would be able to wear the dress immediately as she began to take off the excess weight from her pregnancy. Along with several of Alexis's hand-me-downs, Crissy would have plenty of clothing to see her through the winter months.

The night before Christmas was a festive affair, beginning with a Christmas Eve service at church and ending with a small group of friends gathered around the fire in the living room of the big house. For as long as Alexis could remember, their Christmases had not centered on numerous or expensive gifts, nor on Santa Claus (whom her mother had chosen not to tell her about), but on celebrating the birth of Jesus with others.

Alexis marveled that her mother and father, meeting the sometimes demanding needs of guests nearly every day of the year, still chose to entertain during holiday times. Now that Alexis was older, she helped her mother as much as possible with whatever needed to be done in the big house or around the resort. This year, Crissy, too, had been a tremendous help with baking and decorating sugar cookies and assisting Kate in making little loaves of nutbread to pass out to their friends and guests. But the work was still exhausting, and Alexis, only a month away from giving birth, tired easily.

Christmas morning Alexis awoke to find Cliff already up and fresh coffee brewing. Though she had cut her coffee intake to practically nothing, the flavorful aroma overwhelmed her. She plodded out to the kitchen in her slippers to locate the source of the smell and found Cliff at the kitchen table.

"Hi, sweetie," she said, leaning down and kissing the top of his head. "Mind if I join you?"

He gathered her large bulk in his arms and squeezed her in a gentle hug. "Both of you?"

She threw back her head and laughed. "Yes, *both* of us! For a few more weeks, anyway!"

Alexis sat down in the chair next to him and poured herself a cup of freshly brewed coffee. Savoring the moment, she glanced over at him. "Merry Christmas, Cliff."

His eyes smiled back as he sunk his teeth into a piece of toast.

"How come you're up so early, anyway?" she asked.

"Had to wrap something," he replied mysteriously. "So don't ask any more questions."

She hit him playfully on the arm. "Fair enough. What time is it, anyway?"

"Almost seven."

"Only seven o'clock? I'm so used to getting up at the crack of dawn it's hard to sleep in anymore!" They were due at her parents' home at nine for breakfast and gift opening. Alexis was excited about the gifts she was giving. She'd managed to find a heart-shaped box filled with ten pairs of pierced earrings for Crissy. With all of Crissy's new clothing, it would be nice to have new accessories to go with them.

She was practically bursting to give Cliff his gift, and almost gave it to him a day early. From the sparkle in Cliff's eyes, Alexis could tell he was excited about his gift to her as well. Alexis even hinted at not "bothering to carry them all up to the big house", but Cliff insisted on waiting.

The five of them spent a wonderful day together. After a hearty breakfast of potato-sausage casserole, nutbreads, scrambled eggs, and juice, the family gathered around the tree. A fresh blanket of snow fell outside as Charlie read the old familiar story of Christ's birth from Luke chapter two. They sang several carols, then Crissy began passing out the presents. Each gift was opened in turn, with everyone watching before going on to the next one. When Alexis's turn came, Cliff handed her a large package.

"From me, babe."

She tore open the festive red and green wrapping to reveal what appeared to be a large wooden box. Turning it around on her lap, she soon noticed the thatch roof, four-inch wooden dowel, and small round opening. She squealed. "Oh, Cliff! It's a birdhouse, isn't it?"

He grinned smugly. "Hmm mmm. I know how you like to watch the birds from our kitchen window. Now when you're sitting in the rocker with the baby you can watch them from the living room, too. And look what it says." He pointed to the words carefully painted above the entrance hole.

"Alex's Love Nest," she read aloud. The entire family broke out laughing.

Cliff was eager for her approval. "Do you like it, Hon?"

"I love it, Sweetie," she replied, giving him a tight hug. "And especially because you made it for me." Then, excited, she said, "Now open yours!"

Cliff was equally thrilled with his tool set, saying, "Wow, these things cost a fortune!" He immediately removed it from the box to try out all of the various attachments.

Kate loved the colorful sweater as well as the heart pendant and suggested that they "turn the girls loose in Vancouver more often."

From her parents Alexis received the special chocolates she had loved for years as well as bath powder and cologne. She was pleased and surprised to receive a lovely, dainty pale pink negligee from Crissy.

"Oooh," she breathed.

"Oooh," Cliff echoed, and Alexis pretended to frown at him.

"For when you get skinny again," Crissy informed her with a grin.

After the last of the gift wrap had been stuffed into a box for discarding, Alexis and Crissy went to the kitchen to help with dinner. No guests were expected, but Kate had outdone herself baking pies "just in case". The work paid off, as a couple they had known for years dropped in early in the evening.

Alexis couldn't remember spending such an enjoyable day for a long time. While the men watched a football game, the three women worked a puzzle from beginning to end. In the evening, Kate made turkey sandwiches and claimed the television set, insisting they all watch "It's a Wonderful Life" yet again that year. When darkness had fallen all around, and Alexis was too sleepy to keep her eyes open, Cliff suggested they leave for home. No sooner had her head hit the pillow than she was fast asleep.

* * *

Chapter Thirteen

With Christmas over, Alexis did not experience the familiar post-holiday letdown she had grown so accustomed to. Instead, she set about readying her house and herself for the baby's birth. Due date was two weeks away, and she knew her whole world would soon turn topsy-turvy. Though both she and Cliff were excited about the baby, they realized it meant the end of their honeymoon existence, and that certain changes would need to be made. Her mother had counseled that it was common for new fathers to feel neglected, and, though frustrating, was a valid complaint for most men.

"Give him a little extra loving, honey," she advised. "Let him know he's still number one."

After having nearly destroyed her own marriage, Alexis was grateful for any advice her mother offered, asked-for or not. Her parents' marriage was a success story, and if Alexis and Cliff could be as happy as Kate and Charlie were, Alexis would be glad.

Though she tired easily, she paced herself and scrubbed the house from top to bottom. Crissy helped one afternoon, and together they also sorted out old clothing and other items and finished transforming the extra bedroom into a nursery. Kate had kept Alexis's own crib, which now occupied a corner of the room. Painted white, it complemented the pink, yellow and white wallpaper border Alexis had put up a month earlier. Their one big splurge had been a new baby bassinet, which, thanks to a baby shower from the women at church, was now filled with fresh diapers, pins, lotions, and powders.

The instant Alexis felt a deep cramp in her midriff, she panicked, then remembered that there was plenty of time. Trying to reassure herself, she said aloud, "It's okay, Alex. Your bag's packed, and the doctor is on duty today. Now call Mom."

When no one answered at the big house, she started to panic again, then ventured outside to see if her mother was in the office. Snow covered the porch and steps, and holding the handrail, she took care not to slip. Remembering too late that she could have simply phoned the office, she was halfway across the driveway when Crissy noticed her.

"Alexis--what is it?"

"It's time, Crissy--go get Mom, please!" She felt another pain coming on, and she doubled over and held her stomach.

"Hang on!" Crissy told her, then yelled "Cliff! Cliff!" Several guests turned to see what all the commotion was about, but Cliff was nowhere in sight. Alexis cautiously sat down on a snow-covered step to wait for her mother.

Crissy returned with Cliff and her mother in tow. While her mother helped Alexis into the Blazer, Cliff ran for her overnight bag. Her father, waving from the office, knew it was his place to stay behind and tend shop. Crissy was Alexis's birthing coach, and she needed Cliff and her mother there as well. Cliff drove to the hospital cautiously, taking care not to slide on the fresh-covered snowy roads.

"Feels like we've done this before," Alexis mumbled, then instantly regretted her thoughtlessness at the mention of Crissy's baby. "Sorry," she said quickly, glancing over her shoulder at Crissy.

"It's okay," Crissy said quietly.

When they arrived at the emergency entrance Cliff parked while Crissy ran in to retrieve a wheelchair.

"I can walk," Alexis objected, but was grateful for the relief. Each contraction left her breathless.

After they were shown to a waiting room where Alexis could lie down, Alexis's mother took a chair by her bedside and held her hand. "Let me know if you need anything, honey," she told her daughter. "There isn't a whole lot I can do."

"I just need you to be here, Mom," Alexis responded. "You too, Cliff." Cliff was not doing well seeing his wife in pain. Upon noticing, Alexis urged, "Cliff, why don't you go get a cup of coffee?"

"You can't have coffee, babe," he told her, his eyes wide.

"No, for *you*, sweetie," she said.

Relieved, he broke into a wide grin. "Okay, I'll do that. There's a vending machine just down the hall."

"There's a coffee shop in the lobby," Alexis informed him. "Now go. There's nothing you can do right now."

He needed little urging. "Okay, but send Kate if you need me," he made her promise. After Cliff left, Kate led the three of them in a brief prayer, that the birth would go smoothly and that Alexis would not suffer too much.

"Is this when I decide never to have kids again?" Alexis joked, doubling over at another pain. Crissy and her mother laughed.

In the early hours of the morning baby Kaitlin was born, entering her world with a cry and a scream. She thrust a tiny fist into the air, then yawned, and the entire delivery room staff began to laugh.

"You did it, Hon," Cliff whispered in Alexis's ear. "She's here, and she's beautiful."

"Kaitlin Joy," Alexis said tenderly as the doctor placed the tiny bundle in her arms. She glanced down at her little daughter, long dark lashes framing her dark eyes, and squealed. "Cliff, she looks just like you!"

Cliff, overwhelmed by his new position as father, was beaming. "Yeah," he said, grinning. "But she's definitely got your vocal cords!"

After Cliff wheeled Alexis back to her room, Charlie entered through the open door.

"Dad! It's two a.m.!" Alexis said, surprised but pleased at his presence. "Why aren't you home in bed?"

"You think I'd miss my granddaughter's birth for anything in the world?" he said in a husky voice. "May I hold her?"

Alexis handed her over. Charlie cradled the baby in his arms as though she would break. "Why, she's just a tiny little thing," he said in awe.

"Six pounds, four ounces," Cliff announced proudly. "Ten fingers, ten toes."

Just then realizing that Crissy was no longer in the room, Alexis asked, "Where's Crissy?"

"Your mother took Crissy downstairs for a cup of coffee, Hon," Cliff replied. "This has taken its toll on her. Just after the baby was born, she turned pale and asked to be excused."

"Oh, the poor dear. I wondered if the emotional trauma--"

"Emotional trauma, nothing," broke in Cliff. "It was the sight of all the blood!"

The three of them had a good laugh together. Then, exhausted, Alexis said quietly, "I think I'd like to go to sleep now." A nurse gently took Kaitlin from her,

Charlie hugged her goodbye, and Cliff and Alexis were left alone.

"Sleep well, love," Cliff told her softly, kissing her forehead. But Alexis barely heard. She was already fast asleep.

* * *

Crissy thought the arrival of spring at the harbor was the most beautiful sight she had ever seen. For that reason, when she appeared breathless on Alexis and Cliff's doorstep one evening, Alexis was sure it was because Crissy had found a bird's nest or seen a squirrel.

She opened the door wide. "Crissy, what's up? Come on in!"

"Alexis, I need to talk to you!" Her blue eyes were wide.

"What's the matter, Hon?" Alexis was reminded of the day about ten months ago when Crissy had appeared so unexpectedly in the laundry room at Malibu. The Crissy before her now was a totally different girl in looks and maturity.

"A boy asked me out!"

Alexis shrieked. "Are you going? Who was it?"

"Scott Hammond, a boy from church. Do you know him?"

Alexis shook her head. "No. Is he cute?"

The redhead broke into a wide grin. "You bet he is! And he thinks I am, too! He asked me to go to dinner at the Jolly Roger Inn."

"Oooh, ritzy," Alexis drooled. "How exciting for you!"

"The best part is," Crissy went on, "he knows all about my stepfather and the baby and everything from a testimony I gave at youth group, and it doesn't matter to him! He said he's sorry for my sake, but that it wasn't my fault, and I shouldn't feel guilty."

Alexis's heart warmed. She was beginning to like this boy already. "When are you going?" she asked.

"Tomorrow night. But Alexis, there's one problem!"

"What's that?'"

Crissy's eyes showed panic. "I don't have anything to wear!"

Alexis motioned her into a chair. "Hmmm, that *is* a problem. Maybe we could go shopping!"

Crissy frowned. "Maybe, but I don't have much money. Your parents have been good about paying me for chores, but it doesn't add up very fast. Besides, I won't let them pay me very much, I'm so obliged to everyone."

An idea was forming in Alexis's mind. "You know, Crissy," she began slowly, "I might have just the thing. My banquet dress!"

"Really?"

"Yeah! Follow me." They headed down the hallway to the bedroom. Alexis pulled out a few hangers from the very back of the closet.

"Ah, here it is!" She pulled the peach and cream floral dress into view. "I haven't worn this since last spring," she told Crissy. "It's one of my favorites. I bought it in Vancouver during college."

Crissy's blue eyes widened. "Are you sure you don't mind if I borrow it?"

"Oh no, not at all. In fact, I'd be pleased to have you wear it. But do you like it?"

The teenager nodded eagerly. "It's the nicest dress I've ever seen. May I try it on?"

When Crissy emerged from the bathroom wearing the dress, Alexis insisted she model it for Kate. They left Kaitlin with Cliff, who was just coming up the steps, and walked together up the hill. Entering the house, they found Kate and Charlie playing cards with a couple of guests. The minute Crissy walked through the door, Charlie looked up and whistled.

Crissy blushed. Kate agreed that the dress looked lovely on her figure, slim once again since giving birth.

"I have just the thing to go with it," Kate said suddenly, excusing herself from the table. She disappeared from the room while the guests sat curiously by. When she re-entered, she carried a string of pearls. "Try these on," she urged.

"Oh, no, I could never wear those!" Crissy protested.

"Go ahead, I insist. They'll look lovely with the dress."

Crissy slipped the long string of pearls over her head and ran down the hall to check herself in the mirror. After several minutes, she came out wearing off-white hose and cream-colored pumps, and the pearl drop earrings that were part of the ten-pair set Alexis had given her at Christmas.

Alexis felt a tingle go down her spine. It warmed her heart to see Crissy lead a normal life--school, dating, church activities. Charlie was even teaching her to drive.

The next evening Alexis waited up. Crissy had promised to come tell her all about her first date. Cliff had gone to bed early, and listening for Crissy's steps on the porch, Alexis had nodded off reading a romance novel when she heard a knock at the door.

Crissy was grinning from ear to ear.

"Well, how was it?" Alexis prodded, opening the door. "Come in and tell all."

Crissy giggled. "It was fun. Scott is a really nice boy. He even opened the doors for me! I didn't know boys could be so polite."

Alexis smiled. "What did you have to eat?" She thought of all of the fancy dishes the restaurant was known for.

"A hamburger and French fries. Scott did, too."

"Oh Crissy, I can't believe it! All that fancy food, and you have a hamburger! You can have that at home!"

"I know, but that's still my favorite. Besides, everything else was so expensive." Crissy's blue eyes widened. "Did you know Scott has a part-time job? He bags groceries at the market. After school and on weekends."

"Oh, I've probably seen him before, then. Did you have plenty to talk about?"

"Hmm hmmm. And Scott was really nice, asked me if I was doing okay, after having the baby and all."

Alexis smiled. She was really beginning to like this boy.

"Speaking of babies, is Kaitlin asleep?" Crissy suddenly asked. "I didn't see her much today."

Alexis nodded. "I'm afraid so. Would you like a peek at her?"

Crissy nodded eagerly. Together they walked down the hall to the baby's room and stood in the doorway peering at her. Dark lashes brushed Kaitlin's little cheeks, and her tiny chest moved up and down with each breath under the pale pink sleeper.

"One of the most peaceful sights I've ever seen," Alexis murmured. "I'm so thankful for her."

"I'm so happy for you," Crissy said. "You're very lucky, you know. You have everything anybody could want."

Alexis turned to look at her and was silent for a moment. Yes, she was indeed. Not lucky but blessed. To have a baby like Kaitlin and a loving husband as well.

"You will someday, too," Alexis whispered. "I'm sure of it." She was rewarded by one of Crissy's bright smiles. After a quick hug, Crissy left for home.

Alert again after Crissy's visit, Alexis sat in the armchair reading her book until she felt herself dozing off. She dropped into bed, exhausted, and slept soundly until she heard Kaitlin's cry the next morning. Having a baby around certainly created a whole new timetable. Cliff had already left the house, and Alexis wondered if she would ever get on a schedule she could live with. Accustomed to being able to stay up as late as she wanted, or leave the cabin whenever she pleased, she found it a little frustrating to be so confined.

"It's a happy confinement, though," she told her mother one evening as she sat in the rocker holding baby Kaitlin. "This is my favorite time of the day. She's eaten, she's happy. It's our special time together." The baby's eyes were closed, and her tiny mouth puckered into a yawn.

"The trouble is," she added, her own mouth opening into a wide yawn, "by the time she conks out, I'm ready to, too! I feel like I'm not getting anything done these days!"

Kate's response was touching. "Honey, you're doing the most important job that ever was. And I mean that sincerely. Being a mother is your number one role right now. That baby depends on you to give her things that no one else can."

Alexis nodded. "I know you're right. It's just that...my whole life is so different now! Poor Cliff. He comes home tired and hungry, wanting a little attention, and I'm usually zonked out on the couch."

Her mother's eyes took on a mischievous smile. "Then let him wake you once in a while," she whispered. "Have you worn that pink negligee yet?"

"Mom!" Pretending to be shocked, Alexis burst out laughing.

* * *

Chapter Fourteen

While Alexis enjoyed being a wife and mother, the thought of going back to nursing school often tugged at her mind. Several months had passed since Kaitlin was born. She was a healthy, contented baby, and Cliff a loving husband. But for Alexis it still was not enough.

Why can't I be satisfied with this? she argued with herself. But she knew in her heart she couldn't give up her dream--not yet. A person should be everything they could be. Besides, the Bible said, "Delight thyself also in the Lord, and he shall give thee the desires of thine heart" (Psalm 37:4). The pastor had said once in a sermon that most people thought the verse meant that God gave you everything you wanted. "No," he had stressed emphatically, "it more literally means God GIVES you the very desires, not necessarily gives you WHAT you desire."

DARLENE LUNSFORD

The concept had taken awhile for Alexis to grasp. But in reality, if God had given her such a strong desire to be a nurse, then she should be a nurse.

Now if she could only convince Cliff.

Inspired at remembering the verse, she forged ahead with her own secret plan. First, she wrote to the college for information, then figured up the couple's finances. After that she talked to her mother, swearing her to secrecy. "And pray!" she implored Kate.

Kate only smiled, knowing that God's will, whatever it might be, would win out.

With all that behind her, Alexis paced the floor one evening, nervously waiting for Cliff to come home after a long day of repair work. She had something very important to ask him, but the question must wait for just the right moment. When finally she heard his heavy steps on the porch, she smoothed back her hair and waited.

"Hi, hon. Baby asleep?" he asked, planting a quick kiss on her cheek.

"Uh huh. Did you get that porch railing fixed?"

"Yup. Good as new." He sat down at the kitchen table and Alexis poured him a glass of cold milk. "Hmmm. Got any more of that cinnamon bread?"

Alexis gladly complied. She felt a little like Queen Esther before asking King Xerxes to save the Jews. Her request wasn't quite as frightening to ask, but just as important, at least to her. And she had the same fears as Queen Esther about being turned down.

"Cliff, I--I need to ask you something," she confessed after cutting him a slice of bread and pouring another glass of milk.

"Whatever you want, Alex--just ask." Taking a bite of cinnamon bread, he turned toward her with a contented smile. "Hmmm. This stuff's delicious."

"I--I want to go back to nursing school." She held her breath.

He was a bit taken aback. "Now, with a baby? But how?"

Alexis took a deep breath before replying. "I've given it a lot of thought. It would mean all of us moving to Vancouver, of course--I mean, the three of us. You, me, and Kaitlin. I would go to school, and you could take care of Kaitlin during the day, then get a night job. Or temporarily work from home -- so many people are doing that now! If I started school in the spring, a year from now, to make up the quarter I never finished, she would be over a year old." She hesitated. "But I'd really like to start in the fall. Kaitlin would be eight months old then, old enough for you to watch her without any major hassles--I hope.

"I know it's a lot to ask," she went on. "But--it can work. Someone with your computer skills could get a job anywhere. And now Crissy is here to help Mom and Dad."

Cliff only stared at her, and opened his mouth ready to answer, then seemed to think better of it.

"Please--" she silenced him with a hand to his mouth. "Please, Cliff, think about it." Then as an afterthought, she added, "Pray about it." Alexis knew that the same Father Cliff served loved them both, and He would work this whole thing out so that both were happy. She was more certain of it than she had been of anything in her life.

Alexis had already decided that if Cliff said 'no' to her request, she would be content to remain here in the harbor as his wife and Kaitlin's mother. She knew that was her main vocation in life. She had chosen it, and, since rededicating herself to God, took it very seriously. Who better to raise their child than she? Who better to love this man and meet his needs?

Over the next few weeks, Cliff secretly agonized over the decision. Keeping his fears from Alexis, he instead talked it over with his father-in-law one afternoon while replacing a cabinet in one of the motel units.

"Son, maybe it is time to branch out on your own," Charlie advised. "We certainly appreciate your help, but we don't expect to hold you here forever. You've got your own life to live. Hopefully I won't feel the need to retire until after Alexis has graduated." He chuckled, and his whole face changed into a smile. "That daughter of mine always did want to dissect things. Do you know that one time I caught her trying to give a dead fish a shot? A shot, mind you. She'd found this old needle in one of the cabins after the guests left for home--an

insulin needle, most likely--but her mother had a fit."
He shook his head. "Alexis just said she was trying to
make the fish wiggle again."

Cliff chuckled. "She'd make a good nurse," he
admitted. "And I don't feel like I can hold her back.
Besides, why would I *want* to? Man, I want her to be
better off for marrying me, not worse! Who am I to
keep the woman I love from reaching her dreams?"

Charlie's eyes twinkled. "Sounds to me like you've
already made a decision, son," he told Cliff with a
knowing look, giving him a playful punch on the arm.
Cliff grinned sheepishly, and the two walked back to
the house.

Yes, Cliff admitted to himself, he *had* already
arrived at a decision. If Alexis wanted to be a nurse,
then she should be a nurse. It wasn't her fault that she
had to leave school early. She had done the responsible
thing and came home when her parents needed her.
Now it was time for all of them to give back to Alexis
what she wanted the most.

Having the matter settled in his mind, Cliff
planned a special surprise for letting Alexis know.
Asking Crissy to babysit one evening, he took Alexis to
dinner at the Fisherman's Inn. Alexis, thinking this was
an early birthday celebration, had worn the peach floral
dress she had loaned to Crissy just a few weeks before.
They drove the Blazer rather than taking the Seaswirl,
and Cliff again selected a table overlooking the water.
To Alexis's delight, a single red rose in a crystal vase

awaited them on a white linen tablecloth, the only tablecloth in the restaurant. She felt a tingle go all the way through her. *The setting was exactly like their first date.*

They laughed as they reminisced about that evening--Alexis being late and calling her mother, Cliff giving her the makeup/tackle box. Alexis smiled, remembering Cliff's kiss that night as he left her at her front door.

Alexis had splurged on chocolate mousse and was savoring the last delicious spoonful and sipping her coffee when Cliff produced a small package.

"Oh!" She felt as giddy as a young girl in love. God had not only given her back an attentive husband but had blessed them with a beautiful baby girl as well. Alexis accepted the gift and gingerly tore off the bright foil wrapping, but not before shaking it to hear a jangle from inside.

The open lid revealed a shiny gold bracelet. A Pandora charm bracelet she had admired while on a recent trip to the city. "Oh, Cliff, it's so pretty," Alexis murmured, then did a double-take. "Oh, *Cliff*!"

At Alexis's outburst, several other patrons turned to look, but the two were oblivious to anyone but each other. As Cliff helped her with the tiny clasp, their eyes met and held. Alexis's eyes brimmed with tears, Cliff's filled with love.

The bracelet held a single gold charm: a nurse's cap.

It told Alexis all she needed to know.

Did you read Land of Promise?

Darlene's first published work was a mini-mystery for Woman's World magazine. She has written numerous short stories, including a true experience of helping a homeless couple which was published in a Sunday School paper. Writing has been her passion since childhood -- but as life intervened and other priorities bullied their way, it was forced to take a back seat in her life. Attending OCW Conferences has been a giant BOOST for jumping back into the front seat of the writing world. She primarily writes inspirational romance and meditations but is also putting the finishing touches on a mystery involving Mt. Rushmore. Her first book, *Land of Promise*, was published by Winged Publications in June of 2023.

Darlene and her first husband fostered many children and were active in youth group and camps. Several times they participated in the "Tool and Tackle" weeks at Camp Malibu in Canada. When her husband passed away in 2016, she continued working full-time for a law firm until retirement in 2020. In 2021 she rekindled a teenage friendship and remarried. Now she enjoys spending time traveling with him, writing, reading, and interacting with new people she meets everywhere.

Made in United States
Troutdale, OR
12/18/2023

16044898R00130